PLAY

THE TINDERBOX

Written by:

RALPH C. HAMM III

Little Red Cell Publishing
New London, Connecticut. 06320

Church of All Nations
333 Tremont Street,
Boston, MA 02116
May 5, 1979

Ralph C. Hamm III
(aka Shyaam tangosa Bakuba)
MCI Walpole, PO Box 150,
South Walpole, MA 02071

Dear Mr. Hamm,

My apologies again for the delay in getting back to you concerning "The Tinderbox." Your script has now received several careful readings and we would like to schedule it for a staged reading in the fall. In the meantime there might be some revisions which could be made in the script which would both strengthen it and make it more playable on stage. I have show the script to Jim Spruill of the New African Company here in town who is enthusiastic about the script and would like to be involved in mounting the staged reading. Would it be possible for him to get together with you sometime in June to talk a little more about the piece? I am assuming of course that you would be interested in a reading of the script and continued work on it.

Please let me know how this sounds to you. You have written, I feel, an interesting and worthwhile piece. Look forward to hearing from you.

Sincerely yours,

Steve Lydenberg

DEDICATION

Mrs. Margeret Elizabeth Hamm—my mother; and Mr. Ralph Conrad Hamm, Jr. [may he rest in peace]—my father. For doing such a good job, in their allotted times, raising a Black family in 1950-1970 America. They both deserve Medals of Valor, and Honor, just for their attempt at fulfilling a dream.

CONTENTS

THE TINDERBOX

CAST OF CHARACTERS

ELIZABETH CONRAD
35 year old wife of Randall, and the mother of six children. (Afro/American ancestry.)

RANDALL CONRAD, JR.
38 year old husband of Elizabeth, and the father of four children. (Afro/American ancestry.)

VIVIAN COOKE
14 year old daughter of Elizabeth. Born from a previous marriage.

MELANIE COOKE
13 year old daughter of Elizabeth; also born from a previous marriage.

RANDALL CONRAD, 3rd [RANDY]
The only son, and the first born of Elizabeth and Randall. Age: 11. (In the fourth Act of the play, Randy is portrayed as fifteen years of age.)

GLENDA CONRAD
Second born of Elizabeth and Randall. Age: 10.

CORRINE CONRAD
Third born of Elizabeth and Randal. Age: 9.

BABETTE CONRAD
The baby of the family...age: 8.

MR. LUCIANO
73 year old Italian/American home owner.

MRS. LUCIANO
71 year old Italian/American wife of Mr. Luciano.

IDA FITZPATRICK
33 year old Irish/American neighbor, and a close friend to the Conrad family.

JOLENE FITZPATRICK
14 year old daughter of Ida; also, Melanie's closest friend.
(In the fourth Act of the play, Jolene is portrayed as seventeen years of age.)

EXTRAS (Not more than six children, of various nationalities, between the ages of ten and sixteen.)

Production may require that the dialogue be extended or reduced, or a musical score be added, to fit time allotments and schedules. It is hoped that any necessary renovations, and/or adaptations, will not take anything away from the original dialogue's intent, or away from the original theme.

NARRATION BEFORE THE CURTAIN ARISES

"So, you want to build a home!
Is your foundation sunk on stone?
Because, if life doesn't settle like it should;
time will find a tinderbox where a family once stood...
gone, gone house of wood."

ACT ONE

TIME: August, 1961.

PLACE: A lower middle class neighborhood in a Massachusetts, industrial, city; where big business has moved out. The fabric of the city, and the family, are growing old and decaying. Randall Conrad's search for a home for his family has lead him here.

The scene is that of a front porch to a house. The porch is about twelve feet long, and is an extension from the front of the house. There are five wooden steps leading up to the porch proper, and a wooden railing that crosses the front of the porch on either side of the steps. Beside the porch, on the left, three first floor windows of the house can be seen; also, there is the aluminum screen front door —directly in front of the steps [the porch is three feet deep...from its outer edge to the door]—that leads into the [imaginary] hallway of the house. The house is alluded to be a three family dwelling. On the porch there are two beach chairs to the left of the steps. Left front of the porch, and next to the steps, is a rose bush in full bloom. There is a picket fence that is set in front of the rose bush, on either side of the steps. It runs parallel to the bottom step; running up along the side of the steps to the porch. The roof of the porch is approximately six and a half feet above the porch itself, and two noticeable porch-to-roof posts on either side of the steps. A porch night light is centered on the roof between the steps and the screen door.

The curtain opens to find Mr. Luciano, and Randall, sitting in the beach chairs on the porch. Randall is seated in the chair closest to the door. Randy is sitting on the floor of the porch [what could be considered the top step] with his back against the right-hand porch post — looking at Mr. Luciano and Randall. The two grown-ups are nursing tall tumblers of wine, and Randy is sipping from a small glass. Dusk is approaching.

MR. LUCIANO

[*Speaking to Randall, in his heavy Italian accent.*]

That's a fine wagon you got there. What year is that?

[*Setting his tumbler of wine down on the porch railing.*]

RANDALL

[*Brings the tumbler down from his lips.*]

A '59. I know a used car dealer in Dorchester that gave me a good deal last year.

MR. LUCIANO

[*Rests his head against the back of his chair…his eyes are closed.*]

Ahh! You have very big family…I see the need for such a automobile. I too have a big family!

RANDALL

Oh!?

[*Takes another sip from his tumbler, and reaches over to push his son's head just as Randy puts his glass to his lips. Randy gets some of the wine up in his nose, and pulls away from his father's reach — sputtering. Randy is smiling as he wipes the wine from his face with his hand. Randall sticks his tongue out at his son.*]

MR. LUCIANO

[*Reflectively.*]

Three daughters…four sons! They all married…I've got nineteen grandchildren.

RANDY

[*Noticeably impressed.*]

Wow!

[*Mr. Luciano opens his eyes, and looks at Randy.*]

That's alot of children! I wish I hadda brother.

MR. LUCIANO

It is something! One day you 'n your sisters will do the same for your mother 'n father.

[*Smiles.*]

RANDALL

[*Talking to Mr. Luciano, jokingly.*]
Oh, I don't know about Randy there. He seems to be afraid of girls.

RANDY

[*Defensively.*]
No. suh!

RANDALL

The two older girls chase the boyfriends, but old Randy is too concerned
with his bicycle to notice the little chickadees !
[*Randall, and Mr. Luciano, laugh. Randall reaches for Randy's head,
but Randy ducks under his outstretched hand.*]

RANDY

[*With a whine in his voice.*]
I notice 'em...they're a pain in the neck!

MR. LUCIANO

[*Probing.*]
Does he go to dances?

RANDALL

[*Takes another sip of wine, then places the tumbler on the railing in
front of him.*]
Well, in Boston the Y.M.C.A. is too far for him to be going by himself.
None of them have ever gone to a dance to my knowledge...they all
dance around the house with their mother though.

RANDY

Who wants to go to a icky dance?!

MR. LUCIANO

[*Jokingly...in mock surprise.*]
Does that mean you cannot dance, Randy?!
[*Smiling at the boy.*]

RANDY

[*With a note of desperation in his voice.*]

Oh, I can dance! Huh, daddy?

[*Looks up at Randall for support.*]

RANDALL

[*Noticing his son's plea for help.*]

Yeah…he's a pretty good dancer. He knows all of the latest steps from watching American Bandstand.

[*Randy takes a deep breath, and blows it out in apparent relief, then smiles.*]

Dances by himself, or with one of his sisters.

[*Randall grins, and Mr. Luciano chuckles.*]

MR. LUCIANO

[*Picks up the tumbler from the railing, and takes a long drink.*]

Ahh! As sweet as the roses.

[*Sets the tumbler on the railing.*]

RANDALL

[*Looking at the flowers in front of him.*]

I'm not a florist, but those sure look like some mighty fine roses. Do you do the gardening?

MR. LUCIANO

[*Sighs.*]

No…thatsa missus beautiful handiwork.

[*The stage lights dim a bit, indicating the approaching twilight.*]

She does all the gardening…these days I sit 'n watch 'em grow.

[*Allowing a note of melancholy to slip into his voice.*]

RANDALL

[*Still looking at the flowers.*]

Well, they sure are a sight to behold.

[*There is a moment of silence, during which they all sit looking at the roses.*]

RANDY

[*Speaking to no one in particular.*]
Ain't there any kids 'round here?
[*Looking about the stage.*]

MR. LUCIANO

[*Seemingly awakened from a reverie. He speaks to both Randall and Randy...pointing in various directions to emphasize parts of his statement.*]
Ahh! There'sa plenty children...plenty children! Six Walker children there...two boys, four girls. Boys are big...grown. The rest your age! Langlois people have-a three boys...one girl.
[*Thoughtfully rubs his chin. Then he points out the remaining houses that hold children.*]
Brown's there have-a two boys 'n three girls. Fitzpatrick lady hassa girl.
[*Smiles at Randy, who is listening to him and following his directions very attentively.*]
Let me see...
[*Rubbing his face with his hand.*]
Mason's have-a five sons...one your age. Clayton's have-a two girls. Ahh! There'sa many children!

RANDY

[*Surprised, and bewildered.*]
All those kids? Wow! Where are they now?
[*The stage lights get dimmer — dim enough so that the stage looks hazy in the simulated dusk.*]

MR. LUCIANO

[*In wonderment.*]
That'sa strange. I do not know! Getting dark. Oh, Ma! Ma!
[*After the second call, a voice can be heard coming from the other side of the screen door. The voice is somewhat muffled, so what is said is inaudible to the audience. Mr. Luciano, yells.*]
Ma! Turn on the veranda light!
[*Seconds later, the overhead porch light comes on, and the porch is illuminated in its sallow glow.*]

RANDALL

It's nice 'n peaceful 'round here.

[*Looks around the stage.*]

MR. LUCIANO

[*Looking directly at, and speaking to, Randall.*]

What'sa your work?

RANDALL

Truck driver. I deliver pipes and fittings for a construction firm...take the stuff to the sites they are working on. At night, during the week, I am a watchman at Lowell Tech.

MR. LUCIANO

[*Nodding his head up and down.*]

You work hard! It'sa long drive to your jobs?

RANDALL

[*Looking at Randy, and smiling.*]

Yeah, but it's for the kids. We gotta live somewhere other than where we are now!

MR. LUCIANO

The missus works?

RANDALL

[*Somewhat shocked.*]

Oh. no...no! She's a housewife!

[*Moments of silence ensue. Randy is swatting at what would appear to be mosquitoes...Mr. Luciano and Randall are sipping their wine, and looking out in the direction of the audience.*]

MR. LUCIANO

[*Talking to Randall.*]

Well...

[*Pausing, for just enough time to put his near empty tumbler on the*

porch railing.]
you will like it here! It'sa friendly place!

RANDALL
[*Trying not to commit himself.*]
It seems nice.
[*Sighs into the dusk. His tumbler is resting in his hand, on his thigh.*]

MR. LUCIANO
There'sa playground down the way...for the children. There'sa Boy's
Club on the Common! The schools...
[*Begins to nod his head.*]
both close by.
[*Points out into the audience.*]

RANDY
[*Yawns...slaps his bare arm.*]
These mosquitoes are crazy!
[*Talking to himself for the most part.*]

MR. LUCIANO
[*Grinning.*]
Look...the little one is sleepy?

RANDALL
[*Looks at Randy.*]
Haw...I believe it's the wine!
[*Chuckling.*]

MR. LUCIANO
[*Amiably.*]
Well...how are the rooms upstairs?

RANDALL
[*Looking directly into Mr. Luciano's face.*]
Oh, they're fine...fine! Just what we need!

MR. LUCIANO

Is there much work to be done...before you move in?

RANDALL

A little. I think the back door to the kitchen, and upstairs bedroom area, should be moved closer to the stairs — so that we can use both floors as one family, instead of the two family set up it is now. I'll do that before I move the family down. I want to get outta those projects we're in now... just as soon as possible.

> [*Randy's head falls to his chest. He has apparently fallen asleep — unnoticed by Randall and Mr. Luciano. The stage lights are dimmed a little more, relying more heavily on the porch light for the lighting of the scene.*]

MR. LUCIANO

> [*Stretching his body, while seated in the beach chair.*]

Ahh! Are you going to hire help? I know of a place that does good work.

> [*Nodding his head up and down.*]

RANDALL

> [*Decisively.*]

No, I won't need hired help. I have the tools, and the know how...I can scrape up a friend or two if I do need some help. Thank you for the thought anyway!

> [*Pauses for a second.*]

The wife 'n kids can help with the odds 'n ends...like painting 'n wall papering. I'm sure glad that those hard wood floors up there are in mint condition. It would be a job refinishing them!

MR. LUCIANO

> [*Nods his agreement to Randall's last statement, then his face and voice become stern.*]

Projects are no place for children!

> [*Shakes his head from side to side.*]

You are wise to move! Children must grow...lotsa room out here.

> [*Waves his right hand expansively, to emphasize his point.*]

RANDALL

[*Shaking his head, with a look of disgust on his face.*]

It's turning into a real jungle out there! You can't even park your car in them projects, and be sure that it will be there in the morning when you're ready to go to work!

MR. LUCIANO

[*Sympathetically.*]

Hmm, it'sa that bad?

RANDALL

That bad.

MR. LUCIANO

[*Shakes his head from side to side.*]

It never happens here.

[*Points to his right.*]

Park right in the yard!

RANDALL

The wife has a car, too.

MR. LUCIANO

[*Wide eyed.*]

Oh?

RANDALL

[*Yawns.*]

Looks like the wine is getting to me, too! Yes, she drives.

[*Looks out in the direction of the audience.*]

There's alota room out there.

[*Pointing to the audience.*]

I wonder if we could rent a parking space from the owners? Who owns it?

MR. LUCIANO

Mason family.

[*Points to the right of the stage.*]

They will give you some space…
[*Nodding his head up and down.*]
they are good people. I will talk to them!
[*Pats Randall on the shoulder.*]

RANDALL

The wife wants to know about the schools. How good are they?
[*Turns his head to face Mr. Luciano.*]
Do you know?

MR. LUCIANO

What grades?

RANDALL

[*Contorts his face, in the act of concentration.*]
Four are in elementary school…the other two are in junior high.

MR. LUCIANO

[*Rubs his face with his hand, in thought.*]
Wellington Elementary Community School…two blocks down.
[*Points to left stage.*]
Good school! Good teachers!
[*Nods his head.*]
Cabot Junior High isa long way!
[*Still pointing to left stage.*]
The children here go…it'sa good school.

[*The screen door opens, and an elderly Italian woman walks through onto the porch with a bowl and spoon in her right hand…it is Mrs. Luciano. Randall immediately jumps to his feet, and reaches for the screen door — opening it further.*]

RANDALL

Hello, Mrs. Luciano!
[*Smiling, and looking at the bowl in her hand.*]

MRS. LUCIANO

[*Looks down at Randy, who awakens with a jerk of his head. She speaks with an Italian accent, jovially.*]

I have ice cream for the boy!

RANDALL

[*Shuts the door, and looks down at Randy.*]

I believe he went to sleep on us!

[*Shakes Randy's head with his hand. Randy reaches up for the bowl that Mrs. Luciano is offering him.*]

Hey, old man!

RANDY

[*Smiling, and accepting the bowl from Mrs. Luciano.*]

Thank you!

MRS. LUCIANO

[*Smiling.*]

Oh, you are most welcome!

[*Stands on the porch...takes a deep breath, and looks out over the audience.*]

Ahh! The roses smell so good tonight! It'sa going to be a lovely night!

RANDALL

[*Pointing to his empty beach chair — addressing Mrs. Luciano.*]

Why don't you sit down and join us? I'll sit down here with the ole sleepy head.

[*Sit down on the porch next to Randy.*]

MRS. LUCIANO

[*Graciously.*]

Why thank you...I will!

[*Sits down, heavily, in the beach chair.*]

MR. LUCIANO

[*Rests his head against the back of his chair, speaks to Mrs. Luciano.*]

We was talking about the schools.

MRS. LUCIANO

[*Smiles, and addresses Randall.*]

Oh! They are all good schools!

RANDALL

[*Smiling.*]

So I was being told.

MRS. LUCIANO

[*Reflectively.*]

All our children wentuh them.

[*Mr. Luciano grunts in agreement.*]

They were good schools then…they are good schools now!

[*She looks down at Randy, who is spooning ice cream into his mouth.*]

He will like the schools.

RANDALL

School will be starting in a few weeks. I hope to be pretty well settled in by then.

MRS. LUCIANO

When will you move in?

RANDALL

Sometime next week, I hope! I want to move the second floor door in the kitchen out closer to the stairs. Maybe I'll start working on it tomorrow.

[*Looks over at Mr. Luciano, who begins lifting his head up from its resting place on the back of the chair.*]

MR. LUCIANO

[*Jubilantly.*]

Fine! Fine! Come tomorrow 'n begin!

RANDY

[*Talking to Randall, excitedly.*]

Can I come too, daddy?!

RANDALL

[*Rubs Randy's head with his hand, smiling.*]
Sure... sure!

MRS. LUCIANO

[*Sighs.*]
There are good people here...good people.

RANDALL

[*Tentatively.*]
If I am not being too personal...why are you selling the house if this is such a good spot?

MRS. LUCIANO

[*Smiling.*]
No! No! Good question! Our two sons and family lived upstairs... they went to California in May. All the children are grown-up and on their own. This is too big-uh house...we are too old for the responsibility. So we sell...go to Florida! Enjoy!
[*She pats her husband on the knee.*]

RANDALL

[*Nods his head, and smiles.*]
Yeah, I guess you two do deserve a rest. You've done a fine job here... this is one nice looking house!
[*Slaps his bare arm, in an obvious attempt to kill a biting mosquito.*]

MR. LUCIANO

They buzz 'round 'n bite all night! It'sa their season. June 'n July, nothing! August...there they are!
[*Clapping his hands in the air, then looking into his empty hands and smiling.*]
Gettin' too old tuh catch 'em, too!

MRS. LUCIANO

[*Seemingly perplexed.*]
Where are the children tuhnight...I wonder? Every night they are here...

running 'n playing. Maybe they are at the beach…or at the carnival.
[*Shaking his head, and pursing his lips.*]

RANDY

[*Looks up at Mrs. Luciano.*]
A carnival! Where?

MRS. LUCIANO

[*Nods her head, and smiles at Randy.*]
Down the street.
[*Points to her right, off stage.*]
Walk down there…you will see it.
[*Randy looks at his father, who nods, then he places his half eaten bowl of ice cream on the porch…gets to his feet, and runs off of the set to the right.*]

MRS. LUCIANO

[*Looking in the direction that Randy has just departed the stage.*]
Ahh! To be young.
[*Sighs, then pats Mr. Luciano's knee — turning her head to speak to him.*]
The heart is young…that is all that matters.
[*Then to Randall.*]
Fine looking boy! He will grow bigger than his father!
[*Nodding her head.*]

RANDALL

[*Jokingly.*]
Not too big I hope! I won't be able to do a thing with him!
[*They all laugh.*]

MRS. LUCIANO

No more spankings?

RANDALL

No more spankings.
[*They all chuckle.*]

MRS. LUCIANO
[*Speaking to Randall.*]
What brings you out here looking for-uh house?

RANDALL
The realtors.

MRS. LUCIANO
[*Noticeably puzzled.*]
The realtors?

RANDALL
Uh huh! We wanted to settle in Malden or Medford at first, but every real estate agency we tried gave us the run around. Even when we brought newspaper clippings that advertised the houses, the result was always the same. Either the house was just sold, or the owners had changed their minds about selling.

MR LUCIANO
[*In disgust.*]
That'sa prejudice!

RANDALL
[*Unemotionally.*]
Yeah, I know. It's not a new experience for me...I've faced it all of my life.

MRS. LUCIANO
[*Sighs.*]
So have we.

MR. LUCIANO
[*Swatting at an unseen mosquito.*]
It took us ten years to get-a house!
[*Shaking his head, and pursing his lips.*]
Justa because we are Italiano!
[*Points a finger at Randall.*]

Justa because you are colored!

MRS. LUCIANO

Columbus was Italiano...he discover this...
> [*Gestures, expansively, with her hands and arms.*]

the pilot was colored.
> [*Nodding her head.*]

RANDALL

> [*Showing great surprise.*]

I didn't know that! That is really a new one on me!

MRS. LUCIANO

> [*Still nodding her head.*]

Oh, yes! Oh, yes! He was from Africa. I learn in school...in Italy!

RANDALL

> [*Smiling.*]

Ya learn something new every day.
> [*Then, speaking directly to Mrs. Luciano.*]

Thank you, mame!
> [*Nods his head once in her direction, as a sign of respect and courtesy.*]

MRS. LUCIANO

You are welcome. We learn much from each other, so?

RANDALL

> [*Smiling.*]

So.

MR. LUCIANO

> [*Yawns, then looks at Randall.*]

Did you make a complaint?

RANDALL

> [*Somewhat dejected.*]

No. What would be the use?

[*Shrugs his shoulders.*]

MR. LUCIANO

[*Shocked.*]

Oh! You should! You might not get nothin'…the next guy might! Ya know?

[*Looks over to Mrs. Luciano.*]

MRS. LUCIANO

[*Nodding her head up and down.*]

That'sa right…that'sa right!

RANDALL

[*Reflectively.*]

You've gotta point there. I think the wife still has the newspaper clippings…even some that we cross checked, and caught, a couple of days after we were turned away.

[*Stands up and stretches, then leans against the porch post at the left of the stairs. Looks off in the direction of right stage.*]

The agencies are all written down, too. So I guess it won't be too much trouble to stop in down town Boston tomorrow, before I come out here,

MRS. LUCIANO

[*Noticeably pleased.*]

That'sa good! We did the same.

[*Raises her right hand, and utilizing the index finger and the fore finger, she illustrates a pair of scissors cutting something.*]

Nip it in the bud!

[*A brief interval of silence ensues.*]

MR. LUCIANO

[*Speaking to no one in particular.*]

We need rain…no rain in weeks.

[*Takes a deep breath, as Randall slaps his arm to indicate another mosquito attack.*]

MRS. LUCIANO

[*Looking at the rose bush.*]

I must water tomorrow...'n do some weeding.

RANDALL

[*Scratching his arm, and looking at the roses.*]

They've bloomed nicely.

[*Turns to look at Mrs. Luciano.*]

Your husband tells me that they are all your handiwork?

MRS. LUCIANO

[*Beaming.*]

My pride 'n joy!

RANDALL

[*Anxiously.*]

Do they come with, the house?

MRS. LUCIANO

[*Very serious.*]

Oh yes...of course. Take good care of 'em...

[*A note of melancholy settles into her voice.*]

they are a piece of my heart...like my children.

RANDALL

[*In a serious, yet soothing, voice.*]

They will get the best possible care, rest assured of that.

MR. LUCIANO

[*Merrily.*]

I do not remember when she was not out here pampering 'em!

RANDALL

I can see that alot of care has been put into them. My wife will just love 'em, she is a plant buff herself! Has potted things all over the apartment. She'll have the space now, and it won't be long before she has this place looking like a green house.

MRS. LUCIANO

[*Displaying signs of relief.*]

That'sa good! I nurse them for years...took a long time to make 'em grow.

MR. LUCIANO

[*Nods his head.*]

Umm...long time. Wanted to grow grapes in back...

[*Points his right thumb over his right shoulder.*]

but there'sa no room! The garbage shed took it all up. So, now there'sa morning glories 'n tulips.

[*Sighs.*]

MRS. LUCIANO

[*Closes her eyes, and inhales noisily.*]

They smell so pretty this time of year.

[*The sound of children's running feet on asphalt...the sound of their yelling and laughter...can be heard. Everyone looks to the right stage wing, and start turning their heads slowly to the left - as if their eyes were following the running children. Their turning heads stop intermittently, to the sound of feet on stairs, and the slamming of screen doors. Their heads and eyes make a complete 180 degree turn, turning from the right stage wing to the left stage wing.*]

MRS. LUCIANO

Here they are now! Comin' from the carnival!

[*She seems to becoming caught up in the joy and laughter of the children.*]

MR. LUCIANO

[*Looks at the watch on his left wrist.*]

It'sa quarter tuh eight...their bedtime.

MRS. LUCIANO

Too bad Randy did not meet 'em. They are lovely children.

MR. LUCIANO

Is he comin' tomorrow?

[*Looks over at Randall.*]

RANDALL

[*Looking off stage, to the right.*]

Yes. I'll bring him with me. Here comes the little wild Indian now!

[*Seconds later Randy comes running onto the set, from the right. He runs up to the porch, then flops his body down in a sitting position on the bottom step. He is huffing and puffing. Randall teases him.*]

What are you puffing for? You sound like you just ran a thousand miles!

RANDY

[*Catching his breath.*]

That'sa long ways!

RANDALL

No, suh!

RANDY

[*Nodding his head up and down.*]

Yes suh, daddy.

MR. LUCIANO

[*Talking to Randy, teasing.*]

One day you will be uh track man!

RANDY

[*Curious.*]

What's that!?

MR. LUCIANO

[*Sitting forward in his chair, supporting his upper body weight on his elbows, which are resting on his thighs.*]

A great runner...in the Olympics!

RANDY

The Olympics?

RANDALL

[Sternly.]
Quit trying to be cute by acting stupid…you know what that is!
[Mr. Luciano sits back in his chair, and Randy pouts.]
I think that it's about time that I got you home…your mother have a fit if I don't.

RANDY

[Pleading with Randall.]
Can we go by the carnival, daddy?

RANDALL

[Noncommittally.]
We'll see.

MRS. LUCIANO

[Pleasantly.]
Did you see the children come back, Randy?

RANDY

[Nodding his head.]
Uh huh.

MRS. LUCIANO

They are your age…they will be your friends!

RANDALL

[Glancing at his watch, and talking to Randy.]
It's nearly eight o'clock, and time to go. Say "good night," and then go wait for me in the car.

RANDY

[Stands up.]
Good night, Mr. and Mrs. Luciano…thank you for the ice cream 'n stuff!

MRS. LUCIANO

[*Beaming.*]
You're welcome, dear…goodnight!

MR. LUCIANO

Good night! See you tomorrow!

[*Randy waves, then runs off of the set to the right of the stage.*]

RANDALL

[*Walks over to shake the hands of Mr. and Mrs. Luciano.*]
Well, thank you for your hospitality. I'll be out sometime tomorrow
morning after ten, if that is not too early.

MR. LUCIANO

[*Smiling.*]
Oh, no! That'sa fine!

MRS. LUCIANO

[*Jovially.*]
And you are welcome!

RANDALL

[*Walking down the steps.*]
Well, good night!

LUCIANO'S

Good night!

[*Randall walks off of the set, to the right of the stage. Seconds later,
after he is out of view, the sound of a car engine starting up and driving
off can be heard.*]

MR. LUCIANO

Nice young man.

MRS. LUCIANO

[*Stands.*]

He is at that.

[*She walks over and picks up the ice cream dish and the wine glass from the porch where Randy was sitting, then -turns around and picks up the tumblers from off of the railing. The curtain slowly closes as she is going through the screen door.*]

END OF ACT ONE

BRIEF [3-5 minute]

INTERMISSION.

ACT -TWO - SCENE ONE

TIME: February, 1962.

PLACE: The Conrad family's new hone.

    The scene is set center stage. It is a kitchen scene [in the house, months after the family has moved in and settled down].

    The set consists of three walls, with the front open to the audience. On the left wall of the set, near the upper left hand corner, is an arched doorway that leads off stage [to the imagined TV room, and the adults' bedroom]. Just before the archway, on the floor and against the left wall, is a four burner stove/oven; and directly before the stove—on the wall—is a narrow door [the pots and pans pantry]. On the rear wall of the set is a door, close to the left hand corner, that leads backstage [but is alleged to lead downstairs and outside]. To the right of the door, approximately two feet away, is a doorway with a flight of stairs that lead up [to a supposed third floor bedroom area]. In the center of scene is a kitchen table. There are two chairs on either side, and one chair at both the front and rear ends. At right front stage, just before the larger table, is a small children's table. This table has two chairs, one chair on the left and the other on the right side close to the wall of the set. There is a roaster chicken in a plate on the large kitchen table. There are also a couple of mixing bowls with large cooking spoons in them, an opened loaf of bread, salt and pepper containers along with a variety of other spices, two onions and some carrots and green peppers, and a potato peeler and a small paring knife; all on top of the large kitchen table.

    Three of the stove's burners have pots sitting on them, and all of the pots have lids.

    The curtain opens to find Elizabeth Conrad in front of the stove. She has a pot lid in one hand, and is looking into the coverless pot. She reaches over to the table, which is not too far away from the stove, and picks up one of the cooking spoons from one of the mixing bowls. She commences stirring whatever it is that is in the pot. Elizabeth is wearing a blouse, cotton pants, and over them both is an apron. Vivian is sitting in the chair at the far end of the kitchen table, near the rear wall...facing the audience. She is wearing a dress. Babette is sitting in the chair on the right side and far end of the kitchen table. She is also wearing a dress, and appears to be reading a children's book — which is lying flush on the kitchen table in front of her. It is Sunday—mid to late morning—and the girls have just returned from church and Sunday School.

VIVIAN

[*Talking to Elizabeth.*]
Y.P.F. is goin' onnuh retreat this Friday.

BABETTE

[*Looking up from her book, at Elizabeth.*]
What's Y.P.F., Mummy?

ELIZABETH

[*Turns around long enough to answer Babette.*]
It's the Young People's Fellowship at the church.

BABETTE

[*Excitedly.*]
Can I go?!

VIVIAN

[*With a look of disbelief on her face, and reproach in her voice.*]
You can't go…you're too young! Only me 'n Melanie can go!

BABETTE

Can Randy go?

ELIZABETH

[*Dividing her attention between the pots on the stove, and her two daughters.*]
No. Randy is only eleven…you have to be thirteen, or older.
[*She lifts the lids, and looks into every pot on the stove — one-by one. After inspecting the final pot, she walks over to the table and takes a seat in the chair on the left…near Vivian…across from Babette. Once seated, she picks up the potato peeler and a carrot, and begins to peel*]

the carrot. Babette has returned her attention to her book.]

VIVIAN

[*Watching her mother peel the carrot, asks anxiously.*]
Can I go, Mummy?

ELIZABETH

Where, on the retreat?

VIVIAN

Uh huh.

ELIZABETH

I don't care. How much is it?

VIVIAN

Jus' two dollars for the whole weekend

ELIZABETH

Mmm! That's pretty cheap. Where are you all supposed to be going?

VIVIAN

To Maine!

ELIZABETH

[*Looks up from the carrot she is peeling, with an expression of disbelief
on her face - and in the tone of her voice.*]
Two dollars to go to Maine?!

VIVIAN

Uh huh.
[*Nodding her head.*]

ELIZABETH

[*Returns her attention back to the carrot.*]
Is your sister going?

VIVIAN

[*Lowers her head to look at her hands that are resting on the table.*]
I don't know what she's gonna do, Mummy! If she don't go, can I go alone?

ELIZABETH

She doesn't have to go with you for you to go.
[*Glances up at Vivian.*]
Are you two fighting again?

BABETTE

[*Not even looking up from her book.*]
Yep.

VIVIAN

[*Defensively.*]
She starts it all the time! I don't even bother her! She calls me 'n Y.P.F. sissies!

ELIZABETH

[*Chuckles.*]
Sissies?! Thirteen years old and talking about sissies. That sister of yours is going to be an old woman before her time. Did your brother sing today?

BABETTE

[*Looks up from her book, and answers excitedly.*]
Yup...'n he was good too!

ELIZABETH

[*Jokingly. Looks up from her peeling.*]
Now how could you pick out his voice alone in a big church choir?

BABETTE

[*Nodding her head up and down, assuredly.*]
He stood up by his-self to sing!

ELIZABETH

[*Correcting Babette's misuse of a word.*]
Him - self! Not his - self.

BABETTE

[*Gingerly.*]
Him - self.

ELIZABETH

[*Smiling.*]
That's right.
[*Then, speaking to Vivian.*]
So, he sang solo this morning, huh?

VIVIAN

[*Happily.*]
Yeah, And he <u>was</u> pretty good!

ELIZABETH

[*Regarding the carrot in her hand, and speaking mainly to herself.*]
Maybe he'll keep it up and become a gospel singer when he gets older.
[*Then, speaks directly to Vivian.*]
He's whining about taking up boxing at the Boy's Club! His father thinks
it's all right, but I don't want to see him with a pug nose and cauliflower
ears.

BABETTE

[*Seemingly perplexed.*]
What's that?!

ELIZABETH

What...pug nose?
[*Babette shakes her head from side to side.*]
Cauliflower ears?

BABETTE

Uh huh.

VIVIAN

[*Places her left hand to her left ear, and bends it over it with her fingers.*]
Like this.

ELIZABETH

[*Looks at Vivian.*]
That's right. How would you know?

VIVIAN

[*Returning her hand to the table.*]
I'm fourteen...I ain't no baby! I read alot.

ELIZABETH

[*Tosses the now peeled carrot into one of the mixing bowls on the table.
Gets up from her chair, wiping her hands on her apron, and walks over
to the stove. Checks the pots.*]
Well, I'm afraid of that stuff...fighting.

VIVIAN

He surely can't fight now, Mummy. Everyone picks on him...even
Melanie's girlfriends punch on him. He don't even know how to fight
back.
[*Shakes her head from side to side, as if in pity for Randy.*]

ELIZABETH

[*Picks the salt container up off of the table, and sprinkles some of it in
one of the pots. Speaks to Vivian with a note of finality in her voice.*]
Well, I'm <u>not</u> going to encourage fighting!
[*She puts the lid back on the pot...walks over to her seat, and sits down.
Once seated, she picks up the peeler and another carrot and begins to
skin it. There are moments of silence.*]
How was church this morning?

VIVIAN

Aw right, I guess.

BABETTE

[*Looking up from her book.*]
They told some good stories!

ELIZABETH

[*Smiles at Babette.*]
Bible stories?

BABETTE

Uh huh. 'Bout a boy 'n a lamb.

ELIZABETH

That's nice.
[*Looks at Babette's clothing.*]
Why don't you go on upstairs and change out of that dress before you get it all dirty.
[*Babette closes her book, jumps down from her chair, walks over to and through the doorway on the rear wall of the set, and up the stairs - out of sight.*]

VIVIAN

Where's Corrine?

ELIZABETH

Probably in the living room watching TV !

VIVIAN

[*Her voice twinged with concern.*]
Ain't daddy asleep in bed?

ELIZABETH

[*Unemotionally.*]
She won't wake him up...she's pretty quiet in there. Is one of the ministers going on that retreat with Y.P.F.?

VIVIAN

I think they're both goin'...'n their wives.

ELIZABETH

Umm...that's good.
[*Silence for a few seconds.*]
I wonder where those other two sisters of yours are?

VIVIAN

[*Shrugs her shoulders.*]
I don't know...they should be comin' soon.
[*She picks up the paring knife from the top of the table. Reaches for an onion, and begins to skin it.*]

ELIZABETH

[*Responding to Vivian's gesture of help.*]
Thank you...I can always use some help. Oh, before you get into that, will you go in there and tell Corrine to pick up some of that junk of hers from off of the couch and the floor.

VIVIAN

[*Empties her hands.*]
Okay!
[*Gets up from her chair, and leaves the stage through the archway on the left wall of the set. During her absence Elizabeth finishes peeling a carrot, and starts on another one. Vivian returns, and takes her seat... commencing her skinning of the onion.*]

ELIZABETH

Does your brother have a rehearsal scheduled for this morning?

VIVIAN

I don't think so. Melanie 'n Glenda were waitin' for him when I left. George Pullman said he'd be right down!
[*Sniffles.*]

ELIZABETH

He's been having problems with the choirmaster lately. Did he say anything to you?

VIVIAN

[Sniffling from the onion.]
Who, Randy?

ELIZABETH

[Sarcastically.]
No! The man in the moon!

VIVIAN

[Shrugs her shoulders.]
He don't say nothin' ta nobody 'cept Melanie.

ELIZBETH

[Shaking her head from side to side.]
They're like two peas in a pod! It's as if he doesn't trust anybody but her.

VIVIAN

[Nonchalantly.]
Maybe he don't.
[Sniffles.]
Whew! These onions are strong!

ELIZABETH

[Reflectively. Speaking more to herself than to Vivian.]
I'll have his father speak to him. They don't seem to be as close as they used to either.
[Stops paring the carrot and stares at the wall across from her, as if she is day dreaming.]
He seems to be trying to withdraw from all of us.
[Snaps out of her reverie, and gets back to peeling the carrot. A brief interval of silence ensues. Corrine walks onto the stage, through the archway on the left wall of the set. She walks over to the little table, and sits down behind it in the chair that is nearest the right wall of the set.]

CORRINE

[Rests her head on her arms, on the table.]
Where's Babette?

VIVIAN

[*Looks up from the onion.*]
She's upstairs changin'. Did you pick up your stuff?

CORRINE

Uh huh.

ELIZABETH

What did you do with it?

CORRINE

It's in there on the coffee table.

ELIZABETH

[*Sternly.*]
Now why do you think I asked you to pick that junk up? I surely didn't ask you so you could pick it up from the floor and deposit it on the coffee table!

CORRINE

[*With a whine in her voice.*]
I'm gonna take it upstair inna minit!

ELIZABETH

You better!

CORRINE

I will, Mummy.

VIVIAN

[*Sniffling.*]
You want me to chop these up, Mummy?
[*Referring to the onions.*]

ELIZABETH

If you would.
[*Turns her head towards the rear of the set, looking in the direction of*

the door.]

I heard the door downstairs…yeah, here come your wandering sisters.

[*The sound of light footsteps walking up stairs can be heard coming from the rear of the stage. The door opens and Randy, Melanie, and Glenda walk through the doorway and into the scene. They are dressed in their Sunday best. Elizabeth yells out at them.*]

Keep going up, and change those clothes!

[*The three children take a left hand turn, and walk through the doorway and up the flight of stairs—saying "Hi!" to Elizabeth as they come through the door. Glenda is the last one through the door, and she is the one who shuts it—continuing her journey up the flight of stairs, puffing as if from exertion.*]

You'd think they were old and gray, the way they huff and puff!

[*Corrine jumps up from her seat at the small table, and makes an attempt to rush up the stairs after Glenda. Elizabeth calls her back before she can get out of eyesight.*]

Corrine! Girl, come back here and go pick up your stuff and bring it upstairs!

[*Corrine slowly retraces her steps back down the stairs.*]

CORRINE

[*Sticks her bottom lip out, and begins to whine.*]

Aww, Mummy!

[*Dragging her feet in the direction of the archway.*]

ELIZABETH

[*Very stern.*]

Don't aww Mummy me! Stop your whining…and quit dragging those feet!

[*Corrine walks out of view, through the archway. Vivian is chopping up the onions now, and putting the diced pieces into the other mixing bowl that does not contain the carrots. Elizabeth is peeling a carrot. Seconds later, Corrine appears on the stage, walking through the archway, carrying some books and pieces of clothing in her arms.*]

Is that all of it?

CORRINE

[*Continuing her walk to the stairs.*]

Uh huh.

[*Corrine starts ascending the stairs.*]

ELIZABETH

[*Yells out to Corrine, before she can disappear up the stairs.*]

Put on your play clothes when you're up there, too!

CORRINE

[*Hollers down the stairs.*]

Okay!

[*Ascending out of the scene.*]

VIVIAN

Are you gonna ask Melanie if she wants ta go on the retreat? If I ask her she'll give me a smart answer!

ELIZABETH

I'll ask her when she comes back downstairs. If I forget, remind me.

VIVIAN

[*Smiling, and sniffling.*]

Okay!

[*Loud banging and running can be heard. Both Elizabeth and Vivian look up in the air, as if looking at the ceiling - the floor of the third floor.*]

ELIZABETH

[*Yells.*]

You children, stop that running up there!

[*The noise stops for a few seconds, then starts up again.*]

Quit that noise up there!

[*Then, to Vivian.*]

Go upstairs and tell them to stop that racket up there, before they wake up your father.

[*Vivian stands up—wipes her hands on Elizabeth's apron—walks over to the stairs, and ascends up them...out of sight. Seconds later, the banging and running cease. Randall comes walking into the scene through the archway on the left wall of the set. He is wearing pants, slippers, and a bath robe.*]

RANDALL

[*Seating himself in the chair that Vivian just vacated.*]
What's with those kids...can't you keep them quiet?

ELIZABETH

[*Apologetically.*]
I'm sorry that they woke you up. I fast sent Vivian upstairs to tell them to be quiet.

RANDALL

[*Yawns.*]
And your hollering didn't help matters either.

ELIZABETH

[*Sarcastically.*]
I'm so sorry, your majesty!
[*Jumps to her feet; throwing the carrot that she was peeling, and the peeler, on the table. She walks over to the stove to the pots, lifts the lids and checks their contents.*]

RANDALL

What are you so touchy about? I work two jobs a day, and all I ask is for some peace and quiet on Sunday morning!

ELIZABETH

[*Indignantly.*]
You work two jobs a day!? How many jobs do you think it is taking care of seven people every day...the cooking, the cleaning, the washing, the scrubbing, the running up and down stairs? I suppose this is a rest cure, or a picnic!
[*Footsteps can be heard coming down the stairs. Randy comes down*]

the stairs into the scene, and sits down in the chair across from where Elizabeth was sitting.]

RANDY

Mornin'.

RANDALL

Good morning. What's on <u>your</u> mind this morning?
[*Smiles at Randy.*]

ELIZABETH

[*Picks the bowl of onions up from the table.*]
Gimme those! You shouldn't be playing with food!
[*Places the bowl of onions at the other end of the table. Randall shrugs, his shoulders at Randy, and winks at him.*]

RANDALL

[*Sighs.*]
Well boy, what are you up to?

RANDY

[*Sensing the tension between his father and mother, begins to fidget in his chair.*]
Nothin'…jus' choir.

RANDALL

[*Expressing interest.*]
Did you sing this morning?

RANDY

[*Enthusiastically.*]
Yup! I even sang solo!

RANDALL

[*Jokingly.*]
Hearing your voice, I can understand why you sang <u>so low</u>!
[*Pushes Randy on the side of his head, with his left hand.*]

ELIZABETH

[*Has sat down, and is tending the carrots.*]
Yon shouldn't say that to him, Randall.

RANDALL

[*Defensively.*]
Aw, he know I'm only kiddin' with 'im!
[*Looks over at Randall, who himself has tensed — noticeably.*]
Now <u>you've</u> got 'im worried! Thinks we're gonna start arguin'.

ELIZABETH

[*Nonchalantly.*]
We're not arguing. I'm just pointing out that you shouldn't keep putting him down every time he does something worthwhile.

RANDALL

[*Visibly, taken aback.*]
Putting him down!? I'm not putting him down...I'm jus' playin' with 'im! Can't I play with my own son?!
[*Becoming noticeably upset.*]

ELIZABETH

What you're doing is not playing, Randall.

RANDALL

[*Hits his forehead with the palm of his right hand.*]
Good lord, woman!
[*Moans, then looks around the set.*]
Did anyone bring me the Sunday papers this morning?

RANDY

[*Jumping to his feet. Addresses Randall, apologetically.*]
Oh no! I forgot daddy...I'm sorry. I'll go upstairs and get my coat 'n go out 'n get it now. It's not too late.

RANDALL

Okay, son, but hurry up!

[*Randy runs up the stairs, and out of the scene. Randall turns to Elizabeth, and speaks to her with a touch of malice in his voice.*]
Why are you always jumping on me in front of the boy?!

ELIZABETH

I'm not jumping on you, Randall. I'm just pointing out things to you when you <u>think</u> you are playing. Randy doesn't look at alot of the things that you say to him as your playing with him.

RANDALL

[*In disbelief.*]
What the hell are you talking about?

ELIZABETH

[*Showing no signs of emotion.*]
I'm talking about...when was the last time you sat down and had a serious talk with him? Do you know that he is slowly withdrawing into himself...away from us?

RANDALL

[*Scornfully.*]
You're crazy!

ELIZABETH

[*Becoming excited, and her voice raises an octave.*]
Yeah, I'm crazy! That's why he doesn't talk much to anyone! He has very few friends, and those that he has really aren't worth having!

RANDALL

[*Exasperated.*]
He's only a child, Elizabeth. He's growing through a phase...that's all. We all have 'em...he's no different!
[*The sound of footsteps is heard on the stairs, and Randy descends into the scene. He stops at the door, putting on his coat.*]

RANDY

Is there anythin' else you want at the store?

RANDALL

[*Reaches a hand into his pants pocket, and withdrawing some coins.*]
Here...

[*Sticks his hand out in the direction of Randy. The hand has some coins in it.*]

get me some cigarettes. Do you need anything, Elizabeth?

[*Randy walks over to where Randall is seated.*]

ELIZABETH

No thank you...I'm all set.

RANDALL

[*Handing the money to Randy.*]
Okay, here ya go. Pick me up some Camels...the Globe and the Advertiser...and there's a quarter for you.

[*Lowers his voice...reproachfully.*]
Don't tell your sisters now.

RANDY

[*Taking the money.*]
I won't, Daddy.

[*Walks over to the door, opens it—walks through—closes it behind himself.*]

ELIZABETH

[*Disapprovingly.*]
That wasn't fair you know...giving to one and not to the others!

RANDALL

[*Puts his elbow on the table, and rests his head in his upraised hand. He addresses Elizabeth in a tired voice.*]
Why do you nag me? I'm gonna give something to the others, I just wanted to make him feel special...you said that he's been down lately. Being around all these women could do it to anyone

[*There is a few seconds of silence.*]

ELIZABETH

[*Stands, and goes to the stove to check the pots. Satisfied, she retakes her seat at the table and returns to peeling carrots.*]

Has Randy said anything to you about the Father and Sons Banquet at the church?

RANDALL

[*Head in his hands.*]

Not that I remember. When is it?

ELIZABETH

I don't know what the date is…but I think it's soon.

RANDALL

[*Lifts his head from his hands, and looks at her.*]

Then how do you know that there is a banquet? It might have passed.

ELIZABETH

Like I know most things around here, the girls tell me. And no one said it passed.

RANDALL

[*Sympathetically.*]

The boy must feel surrounded…spies everywhere. Of course I'll go. I'll ask <u>him</u>. He prob'ly needs a boy's night out.

ELIZABETH

Also…the church is sponsoring a retreat to Maine with the Young People's Fellowship.

RANDALL

[*Leans back in his chair, and sighs.*]

What's that gonna cost me? I'm gonna have to pay for this so-called banquet with Randy, unless it's free…and I doubt it. Now this? How much?

ELIZABETH

Only two dollars…four if Melanie wants to go.

[*Before Randall can respond to her, Babette and Corrine run down the stairs into the scene. They are both wearing their play clothes. Elizabeth redirects her attention to the two little girls.*]

Stop running, you two!

[*Randall reaches out and pulls Babette up on his lap, before she can rush by him. He begins to tickle her…she screams in laughter. Corrine works her way onto Randall's lap, and he begins to tickle her - bringing screaming peals of laughter from her. Momentarily, he puts them both on the floor, and they scamper through and archway on the lefthand wall of the set - out of the scene.*]

RANDALL

[*Speaking to Elizabeth, with wonder on his face, and pride in his voice.*]

They're growing bigger, 'n getting heavier every day!

[*His voice changes to one with apprehension.*]

What were you saying about this retreat?

ELIZABETH

[*Engrossed in her work.*]

Oh, I was talking about needing four dollars to send Vivian and Melanie on the church retreat.

RANDALL

[*Sarcastically.*]

They're your children…why don't you give 'em the money?

ELIZABETH

[*Jerks her head up, and addresses Randall angrily.*]

How come every time I ask you for something for Vivian or Melanie, you throw that crap up in my face?! They're just as much yours now as they are mine!

RANDALL

[*Smirking.*]
No they're not.

ELIZABETH

[*Screams.*]
They are <u>all</u> our children!
[*Peels the carrot with visible vehemence.*]
I'm going to get a part time job!

RANDALL

[*Indignantly.*]
Go right ahead.

ELIZABETH

[*Still extremely mad.*]
I am! I'll start looking tomorrow! Then you won't be able to pick favorites among the children!

RANDALL

[*Matter-of-factly.*]
I'm not picking…they're <u>not</u> my children.

ELIZABETH

Okay! Okay, Randall! You're right…they're not yours, they're mine! And I'll take care of them!

[*Moments of silence ensue, during which Elizabeth finishes peeling the carrots, and pulls the onions over in front of herself to complete peeling and slicing them. Randall gets to his feet, and walks out of the scene through the archway on the left hand wall of the set - leaving Elizabeth alone on the stage. Melanie comes down the stairs and into the scene. She sits down in the chair that Randall had just emptied.*]

MELANIE

[*Merrily.*]
Hello, Mops!

ELIZABETH

[*Looks up from her slicing and dicing, and smiles.*]

Mops? Where do you get these names? If it isn't one thing, then it's another, with you!

MELANIE

[*Sighs.*]

Oh, nowhere! They jus' come intuh my head.

ELIZABETH

[*Her face, and the tone of her voice, becomes serious.*]

Why are you going around calling Y.P.F., and your sister, sissies?

MELANIE

[*Coyly.*]

Well they are! Ellen says...

ELIZABETH

[*Cuts Melanie off.*]

Ellen says this...Ellen says that! What do <u>you</u> say?! Don't you speak for yourself anymore?

[*Seconds of silence pass.*]

Why are they sissies, Melanie?

MELANIE

[*Fidgeting...her voice nervous.*]

I don't know.

ELIZABETH

[*Her voice stern.*]

Well, you better not let me hear of you calling them sissies again! Do you hear me?

MELANIE

[*Weak voiced.*]

Yes, Mummy.

ELIZABETH

[*Softening her tone of voice, and returning her direct attention to the onions.*]

All right. Do you want to go on the retreat next week with your sister?

MELANIE

I don't know.

ELIZABETH

[*Not pressing her.*]

Do you know when the money is due for the trip?

MELANIE

Wednesday afternoon, at four o'clock.

ELIZABETH

Will you let me know if you want to go or not by then?

MELANIE

Uh huh.

ELIZABETH

[*Trying to act, and sound, matter-of-factly.*]

What have you and your brother been talking about lately? Is he all right?

MELANIE

[*Confused.*]

Whaddaya mean?

ELIZABETH

Well... he seems depressed and withdrawn,

MELANIE

[*Shrugs her shoulders.*]

He acts the same ta me.

ELIZABETH

[*Reflectively.*]

Umm.

[*Moment of silence.*]

Do your friends pick on him?

MELANIE

[*Cautiously.*]

Sometimes...he won't fight back.

ELIZABETH

Why won't he fight back?

MELANIE

[*Shrugs her shoulders.*]

I dunno, Mummy! Maybe he's too scared...or maybe he don't know how to fight...I dunno.

ELIZABETH

[*Talking aloud to herself.*]

Probably both.

MELANIE

[*Assuming that Elizabeth was talking to her.*]

Huh?

ELIZABETH

[*Looks at Melanie.*]

Huh? Oh...nothing...I was talking to myself.

MELANIE

[*Jokingly.*]

You got money in the bank?

[*They both laugh.*]

ELIZABETH

[*Becoming serious.*]

Don't I wish I did!

[*A note of sadness slips into her voice.*]
Then we wouldn't be having these problems.

MELANIE

[*Concerned, and curious.*]
What problems, Mummy?

ELIZABETH

[*Perks up.*]
Oh, nothing much...nothing to concern yourself with.

MELANIE

[*Feeling left out of something.*]
Oh.
[*Leans back in her chair, trying to look through the archway.*]
Where's Randy?

ELIZABETH

He went to the store for the paper.

MELANIE

[*Talking to herself.*]
I knew we forgot somethin'.

ELIZABETH

[*Finishes cutting up the onions, and reaches for the chicken to begin preparing it for cooking.*]
What took you three so long to get home after church?

MELANIE

[*Looking bewildered, and sounding confused.*]
We wasn't long!

ELIZABETH

Don't tell me how long you were! Your other three sisters got here long before you all did!

MELANIE

[*Defensively.*]

That's 'cause Vivian practic'ly runs home! Draggin' poor Babette, and Corrine, by their arms. Their arms should be a mile long by now!

ELIZABETH

[*Probing Melanie.*]

There has got to be more to it than just Vivian running home.

MELANIE

Well, we hadda wait for Randy after choir. Him 'n Mr, Lowell were arguin' 'bout somethin'. He's always yellin' at somebody!

[*Pouts.*]

ELIZABETH

Who's always yelling?

MELANIE

Mr. Lowell...the Chiormaster! I don't think he likes kids. He never yells at the grown ups!

ELIZABETH

[*Nonchalantly.*]

The grown ups probably don't bother him...you children drive him crazy all the time.

MELANIE

[*Defensively.*]

Oh no! We don't bother 'im!

ELIZABETH

I bet.

MELANIE

[*Purposely changing the subject.*]

Can I go tuh the movies this afternoon?

ELIZABETH

[*Regrettably.*]
I don't know where you're going to get the movie money, kiddo.

MELANIE

[*Her voice expressing hope.*]
Maybe Daddy will give it tuh me!

ELIZABETH

[*Sighs.*]
I doubt that very much...but I guess there can be no harm in your asking him.

[*Looks up from her preparations of the chicken, and sniffs the air.*]
Do you smell smoke?

MELANIE

[*Sniffs noisily, and then shakes her head from side to side.*]
Uh uh. I don't smell nothin' but the food cookin'.

ELIZABETH

[*Shrugs her shoulders.*]
Maybe it's my imagination.

[*Looks at Melanie.*]
Who are you going to the movies with. ..if you go?

MELANIE

[*Counting the names off on her fingers.*]
Ellen, Elaine, Laura, Maureen, Kitty, 'n Jolene.

ELIZABETH

Your father's in a bad mood. He was joking with Randy earlier. Why don't you ask your brother if he wants to go...then have him ask your father for the money?

MELANIE

[*Trying to impress Elizabeth by her courage.*]
I'm not worried...I can ask Daddy!

ELIZABETH

[*Her voice hardens.*]

Didn't you hear me say that your father is in a bad mood? If you want to go to the movie, then do what I tell you to do!

MELANIE

[*Meekly.*]

Okay.

ELIZABETH

[*Looks up again, and sniffs the air noisily.*]

I know I smell smoke!

[*The door opens, and Randy walks into the scene carrying two Sunday newspapers under his right arm. Elizabeth, and Melanie, look in the direction of the door.*]

MELANIE

[*Speaking to Randy.*]

Do you smell smoke?

RANDY

[*Puffing from exertion, and looking around the kitchen scene.*]

Huh?

[*Shuts the door.*]

ELIZABETH

Do you smell smoke?

RANDY

Smoke? Uh uh. Where's Daddy?

ELIZABETH

[*Going back to work on the chicken.*]

In the other room.

[*Randy walks through the archway, carrying the newspapers. Momentarily, he comes walking back into the scene — empty handed.*]

RANDY

[*Walking over to the table, opening his coat, and noisily sniffing the air.*]
I smell it now!

[*Randall comes rushing into the scene, through the archway. He too is noisily sniffing the air. Elizabeth looks at him, along with the two children.*]

RANDALL

[*Noticeably worried.*]
Does any of you smell something burning?

[*Everyone affirms that they do.*]

ELIZABETH

[*Turns towards the stairway, and yells.*]
Vivian! Is anything burning up there?!

[*Running footsteps can be heard. Seconds later, Vivian's voice is heard coming from the direction of the stairs.*]

VIVIAN

[*Out of sight of the audience.*]
No! Nothin's burnin' up here, Mummy!

ELIZABETH

[*Turning to Randy.*]
Boy, go downstairs in the cellar and check!

RANDALL

I'll check down here in the other rooms!

[*Randall rushes out of the scene through the archway, and Randy runs to the door - opens it and rushes out, slamming it shut behind himself.*]

BABETTE

[*Runs into the scene through the archway on the left wall of the set, accompanied by Corrine. She yells to Elizabeth, excitedly.*]
Mummy, smoke is all in the livin' room!

[*Randall runs back into the scene through the archway.*]

RANDALL

[*Nervously excited.*]
Get the kids together, Elizabeth! Somethin' is on fire!

ELIZABETH

[*Yells.*]
Vivian! Glenda! Come down here!
[*Seconds later, Vivian and Glenda rush down the stairs at the rear of the set, and into the scene. At about the same instant, the door bursts open, and Randy rushes through the doorway into the scene.*]

RANDY

[*Out of breath, and coughing.*]
The wood shed in the cellar is on fire!
[*Gasping, and trying to yell the words out.*]
I threw some water on it, but nothin' happened!

[*Randall runs by Randy...through the open door. Seconds later, after much confusing dialogue between the children in the scene, Elizabeth intercedes.*]

ELIZABETH

[*Nervously.*]
Hush up you children...sssh!

[*Now that the set is quiet, Randall's voice can be heard - coming from a distance - issuing through the open doorway.*]

RANDALL

[*Out of sight of the audience.*]
Elizabeth! Send the kids outside, and call the fire department! This fire is out of control!

ELIZABETH

[*Moving, and yelling to the children.*]

Go over next door to Mrs. Fitzpatrick's...hurry now, but be careful!

[*She rushes through the archway, and the six children all rush through the open door. The scene is empty, and becoming smoky. The MINOR curtain closes.*]

END OF SCENE ONE.

ACT TWO - SCENE TWO

The MINOR curtain is closed long enough for the set to be rearranged. Two of the set walls, from SCENE ONE, are switched and the furnishings [props] are changed.

The curtain opens upon a living room scene. The set is a three walled enclosure. On the left hand wall, towards the front of the stage, is a closed door. To the right of the door [approximately two feet away] is a darkened doorway [minus the stairs]. In the left hand corner, its back against the rear wall of the set, is an empty book case. Next to the book case, on the rear wall of the set, is a closet [was the pot pantry in SCENE ONE]; and close to the right hand corner of the rear wall is an archway -with a curtain hanging down from it, attached to the top on the nether side of the set wall. Against the right wall of the set, near the corner, is an upholstered armchair. In the middle of the set, in the center of the stage, is an upholstered couch which is facing the audience. There is dark stained wood coffee table on the floor in front of the couch.

Seconds pass on the empty stage, then a key can be heard being inserted into the door's lock. The door opens, and Ida Fitzpatrick—a young woman in her early thirties—steps through the doorway into the scene. She is followed by the entire Conrad family.

IDA
[*Walking over to the couch, swinging a key ring around her right index finger.*]
Well, this is it!

[*She spins around to face the open door. Leans against the couch, supported by her left hand, and waves her right hand expansively.*]
A home away from home...for awhile anyway.

[*The children rush to the couch and vie with each other over the sitting positions. All with the exception of Randy, who walks over to the sole chair in the room and sits down in it.*]

RANDALL

[*Sternly.*]
You kids, knock it off!
>[*Seemingly a bit irritated. He is the last one through the doorway, and stands in front of the open door. The children settle down and sit quietly.*]

ELIZABETH

[*Walks over to stand next to Ida.*]
Thank you, Ida! I don't know what we would have done without you! We're lucky that this first floor apartment of yours was empty!

IDA

[*Working a key off of the key ring that she has in her hand.*]
Oh, it's been empty for quite awhile.
>[*Gets the key off of the ring, and hands it to Elizabeth.*]

Here ya go! I'm happy to do it! What are friends for if they can't come through in the time of need?
>[*She looks over at Randall, who hasn't moved from his standing position.*]

Don't worry about the rent either! And if there isn't enough room down here for the children ta sleep, I gotta lot of room upstairs! My guest room is empty. ...it has a big double bed, and one of the girls can sleep with Jolene if need be.

MELANIE

[*Excitedly.*]
Oh, can I Mummy...can I?!

ELIZABETH

We'll talk about it later.

IDA

[*Walking toward the archway, and speaking to Elizabeth and Randall.*]
Well...let me give you the grand tour!
>[*Randall walks with Elizabeth, behind Ida, to the archway. Ida pushes aside the drape.*]

This is the kitchen…on the other side is one of the bedrooms.

[*The three grown ups disappear from view, through the archway—the drapery falling back down into place once they have passed through— leaving the children alone on the set. Seconds pass in moderate silence, broken only by the five girls on the couch picking and pushing at one another. A young caucasian girl, wearing a coat, dungarees, and sneakers, comes rushing into the scene through the open door.*]

THE FIVE GIRLS

Jolene!

[*They all jump up from the couch to greet the new arrival.*]

JOLENE

[*Out of breath, and talking fast.*]

Geez, what happened!?

[*All of the girls stand around each other on the floor space between the side of the couch and the open door.*]

All of those fire engines! Wow, is your house messed up!

[*The Conrad girls all begin to talk at the same time.*]

MELANIE

[*Talking over her sisters, who quiet down once she begins to speak.*]

There was a fire in the wood shed! Mummy smelled it first!

JOLENE

[*Speaking in her hurried, and excited, voice.*]

I wuz over at Ellen 'n Elaine's house when I saw the smoke from way over there!

VIVIAN

Daddy tried ta put the fire out, too!

MELANIE

So didn't Randy!

[*All of the girls look over at Randy, who is slumped in the armchair with his arms folded across his chest. He doesn't respond to them, so they*] *turn their attention back to each other.*]

JOLENE

[*Still very excited.*]
The firemen are all runnin' in 'n out of your house over there! They broke up alotta windows over there, too!

CORRINE

[*Suggestively.*]
Let's go outside 'n watch?!

VIVIAN

[*Cautions.*]
Uh uh! Daddy'll get mad!

JOLENE

[*Looking around.*]
Is my mother down here?

MELANIE

Uh huh!
[*Points to the rear of the set.*]
She's out back with my mother 'n father.. .givin' 'em a guided tour.
[*She becomes excited, and begins to shake Jolene by her shoulders.*]
Your mother said that some of us can stay upstairs with you!

JOLENE

[*Looking, and sounding, shocked.*]
Randy too?!

MELANIE

[*Laughs.*]
No, crazy! Us girls! I asked my mother if I could. ...they will talk about it later 'n see.

VIVIAN

[*Looks from Jolene to Melanie, smiling.*]

Maybe I can, too!

MELANIE

[*Unemotionally.*]
Yeah…whoopee.
[*Vivian looks at Melanie, and stops smiling.*]
So you can make reports on us.

VIVIAN

[*Taken aback.*]
I don't report on you!

MELANIE

[*Angrily.*]
Yes you do!

VIVIAN

[*Shouts.*]
No I don't!

MELANIE

[*Maliciously.*]
Yes you do, <u>fink</u>!

VIVIAN

[*Puts her hands on her hips, and speaks in a hurt voice.*]
When? I'm not a fink.

MELANIE

Every time we kids do anythin' you squeal on us to Mummy! 'n she tells
Daddy…'n we get beat!

VIVIAN

[*Looks at Jolene, tearfully.*]
No suh! I only do what Mummy tells me ta do. I ain't a fink!

RANDY

[*Sarcastically.*]
Why don't you both shaddup before Daddy comes in here 'n breaks your necks...'n I'll laugh!
[*Everyone looks at him.*]

JOLENE

What's with him?

MELANIE

[*Shrugs her shoulders, and answers Jolene in a matter-of-fact voice.*]
Beats me. Lately he's been a little loco in the cocoa.

CORRINE

[*Acidly.*]
He's always like that!

RANDY

[*Mocking Corrine's tone of voice.*]
He's always like that!

CORRINE

[*Angrily.*]
Stop mocking me!

RANDY

[*Slurring his words purposely.*]
Aww shaddup!

CORRINE

[*Screams.*]
I won't shut up!
[*All of the other girls hold their ears, after Corrine's scream.*]

RANDY

[*Threateningly.*]
If I break your neck you'll shaddup!

GLENDA

[*Hanging her head to the side loosely.*]
She'll walk 'round like this for the rest of her life!
[*Everyone laughs.*]

MELANIE

[*Shaking Glenda good naturedly.*]
Stop that, you nut! Let's all sit down. What are we standin' up for anyway?

[*The girls walk over to the couch and sit down. Jolene doesn't sit on the couch, but instead sits on the edge of the coffee table - facing the open door. Once seated, she gets up again and closes the door, then sits back down.*]

JOLENE

[*Jokingly.*]
Well, I guess this blows the movie!
[*Looks at Melanie, and chuckles.*]

GLENDA

[*Expressing deep concern.*]
I hope the TV didn't catch fire!

BABETTE

[*Wide eyed.*]
Me too!

JOLENE

[*Talking to Babette and Glenda.*]
You two gotta be kiddin'! Your whole house is on fire 'n you're worried about the TV! Un real!
[*Then to Melanie, sympathetically.*]
What about all of your stuff in your room?

MELANIE

[*With a shocked expression on her face.*]
I never even thought of that! Oh, wow!

RANDY

[*Nonchalantly.*]

Easy come, easy go.

[*Ida, Elizabeth, and Randall walk back into the scene through the doorway on the left hand wall next to the door.*]

IDA

[*Talking, as they walk through the doorway.*]

...through the kitchen, through the bedroom, and back into the living room.

[*Notices Jolene sitting on the coffee table.*]

Jolene! I thought you were goin' to the movies?

[*Randall walks over to the door - opens it, and walks through - closing it behind himself.*]

JOLENE

[*Talking to Ida.*]

Who could go ta the movies through all of this?

[*Throws her arms in the air.*]

GLENDA

[*Talking to Elizabeth.*]

Mummy, where did Daddy go?

ELIZABETH

[*She and Ida are standing behind the couch now. She bends forward and hugs Glenda around the shoulders from behind.*]

He went to check on the house, dear.

MELANIE

[*Pleading with Elizabeth.*]

Mummy, can I stay upstairs with Jolene?

VIVIAN

[*Excitedly.*]

Me too?!

ELIZABETH

[*Unwrapping her arms from around Glenda, and standing up straight.*]
Yes! You both are.

[*Melanie, Jolene, and Vivian scream in happiness.*]

RANDY

[*Sullenly.*]
Whoopee.

[*Gets up out of his chair, and walks through the draped archway - out of the scene.*]

IDA

[*Looking at the retreating form of Randy, and speaking to Elizabeth.*]
What's with him?

ELIZABETH

[*Also looking in the direction of the archway.*]
Who knows. Randall says it's a phase. I don't care what it is...

[*Yells so Randy can hear her in the next room, there is a twinge of anger in her voice.*]

if he keeps going around here acting like the fool, I'm going to beat the phase out of his behind!

[*The girls chuckle.*]

IDA

[*Walks over to the vacated armchair, and sits down.*]
Well, Elizabeth...

[*Points to the darkened doorway on the left hand wall of the set.*]
Babette and Corrine can sleep in there...

[*Lowers her hand, and rests it on the arm of the chair.*]
you and Randall in the master bedroom. Do you have a cot?

ELIZABETH

[*Leans against the couch...*]
Uh huh,.

IDA

Well, then you can put that in here for Randy...store it in the closet over there…

>[*Nods her head in the direction of the small door that is next to the book case…on the rear wall of the set.*]

during the day. Perfect! Don't you think so?

ELIZABETH

>[*Hits her forehead with the heal of her right hand, and stands up straight.*]

We forgot about Glenda!

GLENDA

>[*Comically.*]

Ta da!

IDA

Oh, that's simple Beth! She can come upstairs with us!

GLENDA

>[*Excitedly.*]

Yea!

IDA

Us four girls will have a ball! Huh, girls?

>[*The four girls in question, shout their enthusiasm.*]

Two can sleep in the guest room, and the other can sleep in the extra bed in Jolene's room.

GLENDA

>[*Looks at Melanie, and comments unemotionally.*]

Melanie.

>[*The door opens, and Randall takes a step into the scene — everyone turns to face him.*]

RANDALL

>[*Hurriedly.*]

They're through over there…let's go see what we can salvage!

>[*Looks at the girls on the couch.*]

Glenda, you stay here with your two little sisters.

[*Looks around the scene.*]

Where's Randy?

[*Yells.*]

Randy! Let's go boy!

[*Randy comes hurriedly on the set, through the archway, heading straight for his father.*]

Get over to the house...and be careful!

[*Everyone moves, heading for the open door, with the exception of Corrine, Babette, and Glenda.*]

IDA

Jolene, and I, will come and help too!

[*The seven actors walk off of the set, through, the door...shutting it behind them. Corrine, Babette, and Glenda sit on the couch looking at the closing door. The curtain closes.*]

END OF SCENE

END OF ACT TWO.

BRIEF [3-5 minute] INTERMISSION.

ACT THREE - SCENE ONE

TIME: August, 1962.

PLACE: In the renovated Conrad family home — six months after the fire.

This scene is set center stage in a kitchen setting, very much the same setting as that of ACT TWO — SCENE ONE. The only visible differences are:

a. The stove is different [a newer model];

b. The kitchen table now seats eight;

c. The small children's table is not in the scene;

d. To the rear of the set, in the right hand corner, is a modern clothes washing machine; also,

e. The door on the rear wall of the set is different.

The curtain opens, to find Elizabeth and Randall seated across from each other, at the end of the kitchen table closest to the front of the stage. Randall is sitting on the left of the table, and Elizabeth is seated on the right. Randall is dressed in khaki pants and a tee shirt, Elizabeth is wearing dungarees and a sweat shirt.

RANDALL

[*Resting his arms on the table—hands folded together—leaning forward on his elbows, slightly. He is very emotional, which is evident in his speech.*]

Look, Elizabeth...the house is remodeled, the new oil furnace has only two more payments due on it, the notes on the cars are paid up to date... you don't need that job! You can stay home with the kids!

ELIZABETH

[*Sitting up very straight in her chair, and looking Randall in the eyes - she answers him calmly.*]

You sound, and act, as if I am working full time. The job is just part time work...three times a week for twelve hours. I know that this may come as a shock to you, but I enjoy the freedom.

RANDALL

[*Sits back in his chair, with a look of disgust on his face, and sarcasm in his voice.*]

Freedom! Freedom! You talk as if you're in prison or somethin'!

ELIZABETH

[*Defensively.*]

Well, there are times that this place...

[*Waves her arms, expansively.*]

can feel like a prison. Believe you, me!

RANDALL

[*Indignantly.*]

Now what can possibly make you feel in prison here?

ELIZABETH

[*Angrily.*]

That stove!

[*Points to the stove.*]

That washing machine!

[*Points to the washing machine.*]

These floors!

[*Waves her arms to signify the house in its entirety.*]

And that's just naming a few things!

[*She calms down, and tries to get Randall to understand her point of view — in a quiet voice.*]

Randall...what is so wrong about me having a job? The children don't have to come running to you all the time about money anymore. Vivian and Melanie don't have to deprive you of your drinking money...

[*Randall gives her a side long glance.*]

and I am paying the note on my own car.

RANDALL

[*Yells, banging his fist on the table for emphasis.*]

A woman's place is in the home! My mother stayed home all of her life... she's still at home now, even though my father is dead!

ELIZABETH

[*Screams back.*]

Your fist banging doesn't faze me, Randall! As for your mother, she receives a welfare check every month; and is saddled with that lazy, drunkard, good for nothing brother of yours — Kevin! Maybe if she hadn't stayed home all of her life, Kevin would have been forced to go out and find a job!

[*Randall gets to his feet, lights up a cigarette, and begins pacing up and down the floor - between the stove and the table.*]

RANDALL

[*Calmly.*]

The children need their mother at home.

ELIZABETH

[*Calms down.*]

My working doesn't interfere with their needs. I work at night when you come home...you're here with them. What's to need, they see me all day?

RANDALL

[*His voice showing desperation.*]

You know what I mean!

[*Still pacing.*]

ELIZABETH

[*Raises her voice.*]

No, I don't know what you mean! That's the problem, I don't know what you mean, and you don't know what you mean either!

RANDALL

[*Stops pacing for just enough time to glance at her...speaks authoritatively.*]

The problem is your neglecting your children!

ELIZABETH

[*Her voice sounding aggravated.*]
Neglect! Where is the neglect, Randall?!

RANDALL

[*Solemnly.*]
The neglect is in your being around twenty-four hours day when your children need you! What if they get sick when you're not here?

ELIZABETH

Show me where it says that a mother must be around her children every minute of the day! Show me! If they get sick I call the doctor…when I'm here! Does your dialing finger have a cramp…is your arm broke, so that you can't pick up the phone and dial the doctor?!

RANDALL

That's not the point.

ELIZABETH

[*Exasperated.*]
Then what is the point?!

RANDALL

The point is that you don't care enough for your family to stay home with them.

ELIZABETH

[*Furious.*]
I don't care about my family?! What about you?
[*Points an accusing finger at him…her fury changes to sarcasm.*]
You care so much for us that every spare minute you get you spend in the barroom with your <u>friends</u>! You spend more time in the barroom than I spend in work!

RANDALL

[*Pulls out a chair at the table, and sits down at the farthest end.*]
Quit getting off the issue.

ELIZABETH

That really is the issue! What do you want from me, Randall? Does my working embarrass you in front of your friends... is that it?

[*Randall does not respond, but sits looking at the burning cigarette in his hand. Elizabeth grins in triumph.*]

Yes! That's it! I actually embarrass you in front of your friends!

RANDALL

[*Angrily jumps to his feet, and begins to pace the floor again.*]

No, you don't embarrass me!

[*Unconvincingly.*]

ELIZABETH

[*Motherly.*]

Randall, look...you don't need friends like that. All they want is to appease you for the drinks that you buy for them every single week.

RANDALL

[*Indignantly.*]

Don't tell me who to choose for my friends.

ELIZABETH

[*Calmly.*]

I'm not telling you who to choose for your friends...I'm just suggesting that you be more particular. That's what you're always telling Randy! What's good for the goose, is good for the gander, you know!

RANDALL

[*Sits down in the chair directly across from Elizabeth, tries to reach her through a subtle approach.*]

You don't need the job, Elizabeth. I make enough money! You could spend that work time doing something else!

ELIZABETH

[*Not taken in by his subtlety.*]

Like what? Selling sea shells down by the sea shore?

RANDALL

[*Sarcastically.*]
Very funny! I was only thinking of you!

ELIZABETH

[*Looking shocked.*]
Ha! You're only thinking of yourself! Which is par for the course!

RANDALL

[*Angrily.*]
What's such a big goddamned deal about that job!? You got the job to spite me! So, now I'm spited...so quit!

ELIZABETH

[*Taken aback — her voice, and face, expressing disbelief.*]
To spite <u>you</u>! I got this job out of necessity! It was like pulling teeth trying to get you to support the children's activities! Your friends' drinks are more important to you than your own children's welfare!

RANDALL

[*Sarcastically.*]
Oh, is that so!

ELIZABETH

[*Knowingly.*]
You know it is! Our independence scares you to death!
[*Leans further back in her chair, and fold her arms across her chest... looking at Randall with an expression of content on her face.*]

RANDALL

[*Jumps up from his seat, extremely mad, and walks towards the door.*]
Independence! Independence is it!?
[*His voice wavering with anger.*]
Well, why don't you take those six brats, and get the hell out of my life?:

ELIZABETH

[*Jumps up from her chair, and screams back — the chair that she was*

sitting in falls over.]
I will! You can live together here with your beloved friends!

[*Randall storms to the door, opens it and rushes through—slamming
it closed behind himself. For a few seconds, Elizabeth stands rigid—
staring at the closed door. She then reaches down to the chair on its side
on the floor, and sets it aright. She walks over to the stairway and yells.*]
Vivian! Melanie!
[*The girls voices can be heard coming from the rear of the stage.*]

GIRLS

Yes, Mummy!

ELIZABETH

Hurry up and come down here!
[*She walks toward the archway. Footsteps are heard on the stairs, and
Vivian and Melanie ascend into the scene via the stairway.*]

VIVIAN

[*Visibly shaken...almost in tears.*]
Whatsa matter, Mummy?

ELIZABETH

[*Still angry, and failing in her attempt to not show it.*]
Vivian, go back upstairs and begin packing. . .hurry up! And Melanie, go
outside and get your two sisters, and brother; Hurry !
[*Vivian runs back up the stairs, and Melanie opens the door and races
through the doorway...closing the door behind herself. Elizabeth hurries
through the archway, mumbling to herself.*]
I'll show him... get out of his life, huh!

[*Moments of silence pass on the empty stage. Foot-steps on stairs break
the silence. Melanie, Babette, Corrine, and Randy open the door and
rush into the scene...closing the door behind themselves. They all walk
over to the table, pull out chairs, and sit down.*]

RANDY

[*Looking around the set.*]
Where's Glenda?

MELANIE

[*Apparently out of breath, rasping out her words.*]
In the livin' room...sleepin'.

BABETTE

[*On the verge of crying.*]
Mummy and Daddy were fightin'?
[*Looks at Melanie, who nods her head.*]
Why do they fight all the time?

RANDY

[*Suppressing any emotion.*]
Who knows.
[*Then looks at Babette, raises his voice.*]
Oh, stop cryin' you big baby! All you do is weep, weep, weep!

MELANIE

[*Authoritatively.*]
Leave her alone. Randy!
[*Randy slouches in his chair, folds his arms across his chest, and sticks out his bottom lip - sulkily.*]

CORRINE

[*Crying.*]
Daddy knocked me down on his way out... he didn't even say s'cuse me!
[*Elizabeth and Glenda walk into the scene through the archway. Glenda sits down in one of the unoccupied chairs at the table, and Elizabeth walks over to the crying Corrine — pulls her head to her body and hugs her.*]

ELIZABETH

[*Composed.*]
I want you children to go upstairs and pack your things. Melanie, you

help your younger sisters, and have Vivian help you.

[*Looks down at Corrine.*]

Come on sweetheart, stop your crying.

[*Then, speaking to everyone present.*]

Go on now...upstairs and do your packing!

[*The children get up from their seats, and walk towards the stairway.*]

When you're finished, bring your stuff down here!

[*The children all ascend the stairs — out of sight. Elizabeth watches them go. Randy comes back down the stairs, walks over to the washing machine and leans on it — looking at Elizabeth.*]

I thought I told you to go upstairs and pack?

[*Sits down in the chair nearest herself.*]

RANDY

Oh, that can be done innuh minit...jus' dump my stuff in my duffle bag.

[*His face becomes a mask of worry and concern.*]

Where are we go in', Mummy?

ELIZABETH

[*Sighs.*]

I don't know, Randy. . .we're just going. Your father doesn't want us anymore... he thinks you're all a bunch of brats.

RANDY

Why?

ELIZABETH

[*Massages the bridge of her nose with the thumb and forefinger of her right hand.*]

Who knows, Randy...who knows.

RANDY

[*Walks over to the table, and sits down in the chair directly across from Elizabeth.*]

Me 'n Jack were in the drug store drinkin' Cokes, when Daddy went by into the Lucky Spot.

ELIZABETH

That figures.

[*Still massaging the bridge of her nose.*]

RANDY

Will we be home tuhnight?

ELIZABETH

[*Stops rubbing the bridge of her nose, and looks directly ionto Randy's face.*]

Why?

RANDY

I wanna go ta the Boy's Club!

ELIZABETH

[*Sighs.*]

Oh...

[*Then, speaking aloud to herself.*]

Our whole life is on the verge of falling apart, and he worries about the Boy's Club. I wish all of life would stay that simple.

RANDY

[*Looks strangely at Elizabeth.*]

Huh?

ELIZABETH

Nothing...nothing.

[*The sound of footsteps descending stairs is heard, and both Elizabeth and Randy turn their attention to the stairway. Vivian walks down the stairs, into the scene, carrying two medium sized suitcases. Vivian carries the suitcases over to the table, and places them on the floor next to the right hand wall of the set. She then takes a seat at the table.*]

VIVIAN

[*Trying desperately to appear happy.*]

All packed, Mums!

ELIZABETH
[*Takes a deep breath, and smiles at Vivian.*]
Good girl! How is Melanie doing with the little ones?
VIVIAN
[*Moodily.*]
She's doin' okay.

ELIZABETH
[*Her voice hardening.*]
Why aren't you helping her?

VIVIAN
[*Sulkily.*]
She said she didn't need my help!

ELIZABETH
What...are you two fighting again?
[*Rests her elbows on the table, and her head in her hands...in an exasperated voice.*]
That's all I need.

VIVIAN
[*Defensively.*]
She starts it all the time! I don't do anythin' to her! She hates me!

ELIZABETH
[*Wearily.*]
She doesn't hate you.

VIVIAN
Are we leavin', Mummy?

ELIZABETH
[*Sighs.*]
The more I think about it...

[Pauses in reflection.]
Oh, I don't know!
[Looks at Randy, and addresses him rather brusquely.]
Boy. Go on upstairs and get your things together!

RANDY

[Gets to his feet.]
Okay.
[Walks over to the stairs, and ascends the steps — out of the scene.]

VIVIAN

[Worried.]
Daddy don't want us no more?

ELIZABETH

[Shakes her head from side to side.]
I don't know what that man wants, to tell you the truth.
[Looks towards the door.]
That sounds like your father coming now...go on upstairs and do something!
[Vivian gives Elizabeth a wide eyed stare, then jumps to her feet and rushes up the stairs — out of sight. The door opens, and Randall walks into the scene... he slams the door shut behind himself. Randall walks over to the washing machine and leans on it. He notices the suitcases on the floor, and grins.]

RANDALL

[Obviously drunk...smirking at Elizabeth, and speaks to her with a slur in his voice.]
When you go...jus' take your two 'n leave my four here!

ELIZABETH

[Trying to keep her anger under control, but screaming nonetheless.]
What do you mean <u>my</u> two and <u>your</u> four!? They're <u>all</u> mine! I carried <u>all</u> of them around inside of me for nine months...and gave birth to them! Now all of a sudden it's your four! A few minutes ago they were <u>all</u> brats!

RANDALL

[*Attempts to stand up straight, but decides against — reestablishing his leaning position on the washing machine.*]
I had somethin' ta do with four of 'em!

ELIZABETH

[*Extremely upset, and screaming.*]
And I had something to do with <u>all</u> of them!

RANDALL

[*Looks around the set.*]
Where are they? Ask <u>mine</u> if they want to stay with me! Go ahead…ask 'em…I dare you!

ELIZABETH

[*Trying to talk Randall out of an apparent folly.*]
Don't bother the children, Randall. You'll just get your feelings hurt.

RANDALL

[*Forces himself up to a standing position, and walks over to the stairway — yells*]
Randy! Glenda! Babette! Corrine! Come down here!
[*He turns around, smiles viciously at Elizabeth, and walks back over to the washing machine - resuming his leaning position. Moments of silence ensure, then the sound of footsteps can be heard on the stairs. Randy, Glenda, Corrine, and Babette come down the stairs into the scene. They all cluster together at the rear of the set; anxiously looking from Elizabeth, who is still seated at the table calmly looking at them, over to Randall, whose expression is one bordering on anger and joviality.*]
If ya'll hadda choice…who would ya wanna be with…me or your mother?
[*The four children look at one another with uncertainty. Corrine and Babette begin to cry.*]

ELIZABETH

[*The dilemma that her children are faced with is obviously affecting her, her tone of voice stresses that concern.*]

Randall, don't ask them that! Look at them!

RANDALL

[*Smirking, addresses Elizabeth.*]
Whatsa matter...ya worried 'bout what they'll say?!
[*Then to the four children, his voice becomes stern, and the alcohol takes a more noticeable affect on him.*]
Well! Who do ya wanna be with...me or ya mother?! Randy!

RANDY

[*Showing visible signs of confusion, and fear...squeaks out.*]
Mummy.

RANDALL

[*Furious. Looks at the three girls; makes a move to stand up straight, and screams.*]
Whadda 'bout you three?! Do ya agree with ya brother?!
[*All three girls are crying now, and they nod their heads up and down signifying an affirmative. Randall makes a threatening move towards them...screams.*]
Get outta here!
[*The four children, in fear, scramble up the stairs and out of sight.*]

ELIZABETH

[*Angrily.*]
You are really stupid! I didn't really know how dumb you were until just now...scaring them children like that! They'll hate you for a long time for that, Randall!

RANDALL

[*Walks over to the stairway. Looks over at Elizabeth, and points an accusing finger at her. Screams.*]
You poisoned 'em! You poisoned 'em against me!

ELIZABETH

[*Sadly.*]
I don't have to say a word to them, Randall. Your liquor does the talking.

They have eyes and ears you know. They're not stupid, either.

[*Randall walks over to the door, and Elizabeth gets up from her chair and heads for the stairway.*]

RANDALL
[*With his hand on the door knob…whirls around and screams.*]
You dirty witch! Keep 'em! Keep all of the lil' bastards!
[*Spits out the last word. Elizabeth becomes enraged. She notices the suitcases against the right hand wall of the set, and runs over picks one up. Randall has the door open, and has his body halfway through the door, when Elizabeth throws the suitcase at him. Randall quickly slams the door behind himself, and the suitcase bounces off of the door. Elizabeth stands on the stage looking at the closed door, panting…her chest is heaving up and down. The MINOR curtain closes.*]

END OF SCENE ONE

ACT THREE - SCENE TWO

The MINOR curtain opens. The stage is set in the same scenery as in SCENE ONE, with the exception that the suitcases are no longer on the stage.

None of the actors are on the set when the curtain opens. After a few seconds, Randall walks into the scene, dressed in jacket and pants, through the archway on the left-hand wall of the set. He is carrying a suitcase in either hand. He places the suitcases on the floor in the corner near the door. After setting the two suitcases down, he turns and retreats from the scene through the archway. Moments later he returns, via the archway, carrying a large closed cardboard box in his arms - on top of which is two pairs of shoes. He places the box on the floor next to the suitcases, and walks out of the scene the way that he came. Seconds, later, Elizabeth walks into the scene through the archway carrying an empty clothes basket. She walks over to the washing machine, and places the basket on the floor in front of the machine. She is wearing a pair of slacks, and a blouse, over which is an apron. After setting the basket on the floor, she takes a seat in the solitary chair that is at the head of the table -close to the washing machine. She is seated there for only a few seconds before Randall comes walking into the scene, through the archway. Randall is carrying some hangered clothes in his right hand, and a pair of shoes in his left hand. Coming out of the archway, he places the shoes on the floor near the cardboard box, and walks over to the table with the clothes. He lays the clothes on top of the table...pulls out a chair on the left hand side, near the head of the table, and sits down. Elizabeth has been following his movements, with her eyes, since he walked into the scene.

ELIZABETH

[*Searchingly.*]

Are you sure you want to go through with this?

RANDALL

[*Sighs.*]

Well... I think that I have to now. I made a damn fool out of myself yesterday, and over the past few years our relationship has gotten steadily worse.

ELIZABETH

You never bowed to pressures before.

RANDALL

You know yourself, Elizabeth. . .that one of these days one of us might kill the other in anger.

[*Throws his arms up in the air.*]

Who knows? I do some crazy things when I drink, and there is always a fight, and we don't seem willing to stop...so.

ELIZABETH

[*Sighs.*]

You're right there. That would be all the children would need to see - one of us seriously hurt the other. Although I must admit that there isn't much that they haven't seen happen over the years! What really happened to us, Randall?

RANDALL

[*Reflectively.*]

Oh, so many things mingled with other things. It's so complex that it's hard to break down.

ELIZABETH

It all seems to have started after Babette was born, when we decided that we didn't want anymore children.

RANDALL

Maybe subconsciously I thought that six children were too much to handle...I don't know.

[*Places his elbows on the table, and his head in his hands.*]

ELIZABETH

[*Sadly.*]

It seems that Babette symbolizes the last of our love for each other. We

died when she was born!
> [*Randall and Elizabeth lock in an eye to eye communication of silence, for a few seconds.*]

RANDALL

Or we realized that we had a job ahead of us, and resented each other for it.
> [*Sighs.*]

Hopefully, you can succeed alone where together we failed. I can't go on the way we have been going, and neither can you.

ELIZABETH

> [*Suspiciously.*]

You talk as if this is a divorce! This is only a brief separation!

RANDALL

> [*Unemotionally, and noncommittally.*]

Umm.

ELIZABETH

What do you mean...umm?

RANDALL

> [*Pleading.*]

Please.. .let's not start. I said umm, because I had nothing better to say - and I was thinking of somethin'. Of course it is just a separation!

ELIZABETH

> [*Relieved.*]

I'll go down to personnel tomorrow, and apply for a full time job.

RANDALL

Do you think you'll get it?

ELIZABETH

Sure! They have openings on the late shift. Plus I'm already a part time employee of the company. That alone should be a guarantee. Are you going to keep both your jobs?

RANDALL

[*Stretches his body while seated in the chair, then rests his head against the back of his chair.*]
Oh, I don't know. Depends on alot of things. I'll send money home to you all every week though, no matter what I decide to do.

ELIZABETH

What about the home improvement loans we made?

RANDALL

I'll take care of 'em...don't worry.

ELIZABETH

[*Looking at the box and the suitcases on the floor.*]
Have you got everything you'll need?

RANDALL

[*Turns his head to look at the things on the floor.*]
No...there are a few more items I'm goin' to take with me. The things that I won't be needin' I'll leave here.

ELIZABETH

[*Gets up out of her chair, and walks over to the washing machine.*]
Let me get these wet clothes out of here.
[*She opens the top of the washing machine, and begins to extract the damp clothing from the machine... placing the clothes in the basket that is on the floor in front of the machine.*]

RANDALL

[*Leans forward in his chair, resting his elbows on the table.*]
How come every tine I want to talk to you, you have something else to do?

ELIZABETH

What makes you think that I can't work and talk at the same time? If I don't do this now there is no one else who is going to do it. We don't have a maid, you know!

RANDALL

[*Sarcastically.*]
Funny! Funny! Funny! You should get a job in a circus...as a clown!

ELIZABETH

[*Scornfully.*]
I guess I should, huh? I've been your clown for years, so I've got the experience!

RANDALL

[*Jumps to his feet, his voice reverberating with, anger.*]
Well, you sure as hell are going to get your wish!
[*Walks towards the archway.*]

ELIZABETH

What wish, pray tell?

RANDALL

[*On his way through the archway.*]
Being independent!
[*Walks out of the scene.*]

ELIZABETH

[*Infuriated. Throws the clothes that she is pulling out of the machine into the basket on the floor. Screams at the empty stage.*]
You never want to take the responsibility for your actions! It's always my fault...never yours! Mr. Know-it-all...goody-goody two shoes! You ought to listen to yourself sometime!

RANDALL

[*Walks back into the scene, through the archway, and sits down in the chair he had previously vacated.*]
I listen to myself all of the time, especially when I am talking to you. When I talk to you it's like talking to a wall, so I must be talking to

myself.

[*Moments of silence ensue.*]

ELIZABETH

You taking the wagon?

RANDALL

[*Possessively.*]
It's in my name! The other one is in your name! Anyway, I'll need the wagon to carry my stuff.

[*Randall gets up from his chair again, and walks off of the set through the archway. He comes back a few seconds later, carrying an open beer can in his left hand, and a lit cigarette in his right hand. He puts the can of beer down on the top of the table, and sits down in the chair.*]

ELIZABETH

[*Turns from what she is doing at the machine to face Randall.*]
Are you going to say goodbye to the children before you leave?

RANDALL

[*Picks up the can of beer, and takes a sip from it.*]
I don't think so. They could care less anyway. They're too young to understand the situation anyway.

ELIZABETH

[*Returns her attention back to the wash in the machine.*]
You maybe right about them not understanding it, but not saying goodbye to them may have a lasting affect on their minds.

RANDALL

[*Sarcastically.*]
You and your lasting affects!

ELIZABETH

[*Turns around to face Randall, with a tone of disbelief in her voice.*]

You really don't believe that the things that they have seen us do to each other...all of the things that we've said to one another...will not show up in them when they get older?

> [*Randall gives her a look of disgust, then picks up his can of beer and takes a drink. Elizabeth eyes him with a look of contempt on her face, that is carried over in the tone of her voice.*]

That's your problem now! Facing life with a drink in your hand!

RANDALL

> [*Takes the can from his lips, and places it on the table. He addresses Elizabeth indignantly.*]

You call this life, and I call it hell! In a few minutes you won't have to see a drink in this hand anymore, 'cause I won't be here! You'll have ta find a new whippin! post!

ELIZABETH

> [*Shocked.*]

You! A whipping post! If anyone's been a whipping post around here it's been me and the children! Boy, you sure come out with some strange things when you're drinking!

RANDALL

> [*Defensively.*]

I've only had one can of beer today! One can has no effect on me! And, what I said was the truth...not strange!]

ELIZABETH

> [*Sarcastically.*]

Right, Randall...anything you say.

> [*She points to the can of beer.*]

You had better get going before you get too many of those in you.

RANDALL

> [*Indignantly.*]

Now you are throwing me out! Can't get me out quick enough, huh?

> [*He jumps to his feet.*]

I have to get the rest of my things, then I'll be gone!

[*Walks off of the set via the archway. Elizabeth is still extracting clothes from the washing machine. A few moments later, Randall comes back into the scene, through the archway.*]

I'm not going to take the rest of that stuff.

[*Walks over to the table and picks up his hangered clothes. Walks over to the door—opens it and steps through the doorway—closing the door behind himself. Curtain closes.*]

END OF SCENE TWO

ACT FOUR

TIME: November, 1965

PLACE: The front porch of the Conrad family home, three years after Elizabeth and Randall separated.

The curtain opens, revealing the porch scene that was utilized in ACT ONE. The only visible differences in this scene, in comparison to the way it looked in ACT ONE, are:

a. The rose bush is not in bloom, and

b. The wooden door is closed behind the screen door, and this wooden door is noticeable to the audience.

Randy, now three years older at age fifteen, is sitting on the top step of the porch with his back resting against the right-hand porch post. He is wearing a turtle neck sweater, pants, shoes, and a coat. As he sits there alone, for a minute or so, various neighborhood children walk by (EXTRAS between the ages of ten and sixteen) in pairs, and by themselves. Randy exchanges greetings with them. The last person to walk by is Jolene Fitzpatrick, who enters the scene from the left. She stops in front of the porch, to the left of the steps, and rests her left foot on top of the first step.

JOLENE

(Amiably.)

Hello, Randy!

RANDY

(Smiles, good naturedly.)

Hiya, JoJo! What's up!

JOLENE

(Emphatically.)

Everythin' is uptight…clear outta sight! Where's Melanie?

RANDY

(*Thoughtfully.*)

I couldn't tell ya! The last time that I saw her was about twenty minutes ago...she was headed for Ellen 'n Elaine's!

JOLENE

Well...she ain't over there! I jus' came from there!

RANDY

Maybe she ran intuh Tony...her ol' man? He was cruisin' 'round here earlier.

JOLENE

(*Reflectively.*)

Maybe.

(*A few seconds pass in silence.*)

He don't get along too well with your mother, huh?

RANDY

Nope! Not many of the kids do.

JOLENE

(*Chuckles.*)

Ya sure gotta point there!

RANDY

(*Grins.*)

Sometimes I pity poor Tony.

JOLENE

Your mother was tellin' my mother that you won some basketball medals...'n trophies... 'n stuff!

RANDY

(*Trying to act as if the awards were nothing special.*)

Yeah, it's no big thang tho'...foul shootin' . . .most valuable player... 'n medals for the first place team.

JOLENE

Are you stayin' home for good this time?

RANDY

Naw. I'm jus' home for Thanksgivin'. I got four days holiday. I gotta go back Sunday night.

JOLENE

How long ya got left there?

RANDY

(*Shifting his sitting position.*)

Another year at the most! I'm try in ta get a scholarship to a private school out there. They gotta outta sight basketball team at their school, 'n I know most of the kids that go there,

JOLENE

(*Turns her head to look off stage to the left — Randy follows her gaze.*)

I've gotta find your sister:

(*Turns her head back in Randy's direction.*)

She disappears quicker 'n anyone I know!

RANDY

(*Concerned.*)

What's the big deal?

JOLENE

Oh nuttin'…jus' the dance tuhnight at the church. I wanna know if she got the money ta go yet! I might needa loan!

(*A couple more children walked by in front of the porch, from right stage to left stage. Everyone exchange greetings with each other.*)

RANDY

(*Trying to impress Jolene.*)

If she don't get it from Ma, I'll give it ta her. I've got enough!

JOLENE

(*Excitedly.*)

Oh? Maybe you can pay my way, too!

RANDY

Sure...I'll take ya! We can all go ta the pizza joint after!

JOLENE

(*Very excited.*)

Great! Outta sight! You must have struck it rich! What did ya do...stick up a bank on your way home this mornin'

(*They both laugh.*)

RANDY

(*With a note of pride in his voice.*)

Naw! I play cards with the guys at the trainin' school the day before we all go home! They smuggle the money in, 'n I beat 'em outta it!

(*Smiles.*)

JOLENE

(*Sheepishly.*)

How mucha got?

RANDY

Oh...'round fifty-six bucks.

JOLENE

(*Displaying great surprise, her mouth hanging open before she speaks.*)

Fifty-six bucks! Wow!

(*Then jokingly.*)

Let's get married!

(*They both laugh.*)

RANDY

This is chunp change! Usually I end up with over a hundred bucks! But I feel sorry for the chumps 'n give some of their money back to 'em for the holidays. I'm jus' an ol' softie I guess!

JOLENE
(Walks up the porch steps, and sits down next to Randy.)
What about your girlfriend…Virginia?
(Looks Randy in the face, and grins.)
Won't she be mad if you take me ta the dance instead of her?

RANDY
(Puffs up his chest, and adopts an air of arrogance.)
Later for her! You're part of the fam'ly…like one of my sisters! If she don't like it, then she can lump it! The Marvelettes said there are too many fish in the sea! So why worry, right?

JOLENE
(Laughs.)
Right! But I sure wanna see her face! She's gonna be smokin'!

RANDY
She don't have nothin' ta be smokin' about! But you're right…knowin' her!

JOLENE
What about Vivian…is she goin'?

RANDY
(Shrugs his shoulders.)
Don't ask me! She's liable ta do anythin'. I'll pay her way if she wants ta go!

JOLENE
(Becomes excited, snaps her fingers.)
That's where Melanie is!

RANDY
(Dumbfounded.)
Where?
(Looks around the set.)

JOLENE

She's tryin' ta get Tony ta take her ta the dance!
(*She grabs Randy's arm.*)
That'll get us all a ride!
(*Widens her eyes.*)

RANDY

(*Indignantly.*)
The chump was goin' ta give me a ride anyway!

JOLENE

(*Teasing Randy.*)
Oh! Bump us, huh?

RANDY

(*Defensively.*)
Oh no, no! You know me better 'n that! I meant we...us...all of us!

JOLENE

(*Shakes his arm, and laughs.*)
I was jus' messin' with ya!
(*Changes her expression, and tone of voice, to one of disbelief.*)
Hey, Melanie told me ya know karate...like Kato on the "Green Hornet"!
Really?

RANDY

(*Seeming embarrassed.*)
Yeah...I know a little. I was tryin' ta teach Melanie some!

JOLENE

Who taught ya? Ya got some books or somethin'?

RANDY

Naw! Ya can't learn from books! This older dude comes from a rich school, on the Big Brother Program, 'n teaches me four times a week. He's Korean, 'n really good! As good as Kato!

JOLENE

(*Noticeably impressed.*)

Wow! Show me some?

RANDY

Not now Jo, I'm not in the mood! If I don't warm up first I'll tear a muscle or somethin', plus I don't wanna get all sweaty. I'll show ya some later on.

JOLENE

Okay! I'm gonna call ya up on that.

(*She stands up and looks to the left of the stage. Randy stands up and does the same.*)

There they are now!

RANDY

She's callin' ya…wavin'.

JOLENE

(*Rushing down the stairs.*)

Remember…we gotta date tuhnight!

RANDY

(*Chuckles.*)

Don't worry…I won't forget!

JOLENE

(*Running towards the left stage wing, she yells over her shoulder to Randy.*)

Later!

(*She rushes out of the scene. Randy sits back down on the porch. A few moments pass, then Glenda walks into the scene from left stage.*)

GLENDA

(*Stops at the foot of the stairs of the porch, and addresses Randy excitedly.*)

Daddy's upstairs! He's comin' down ta talk ta you!

RANDY

(Unemotionally.)
Whoopee.
(Twirls the index finger of his right hand in the air. Glenda runs out of the scene in the direction of right stage. Seconds of silence pass, then the lock on the wooden front door can heard being turned. The door opens, then the screen door is opened, and Randall walks through onto the porch. He closes both of the doors behind himself, and takes a seat on the porch next to Randy.)

RANDALL

(Looks at Randy.)
Mind if I sit down?

RANDY

(Nonchalantly.)
No, I don't mind. It ain't nothin' ta me.

RANDALL

I hear you've been playin' ball? Stockin' up quite a collection of trophies, huh?

RANDY

(Distantly.)
Yeah…I guess so.

RANDALL

(Trying to bridge the gap between himself and his son.)
What's this I hear about you takin' up karate? How long have you been doin' that?

RANDY

(Showing some emotion…disdain.)
Since you left 'n they put me away in the trainin' school… for over two years! A Korean friend of mine comes down to the school I am at from the Academy he goes to…on the Big Brother Program. While the kids

are wrestlin' in the gym, he takes me in the other room 'n teaches me Tae Kwon Do.

(*Becomes more enthusiastic.*)

His father is a Grand Master!

RANDALL

(*Noticing that he has got his son talking, tries to keep the conversation alive.*)

What's a Grand Master?

RANDY

It's a guy that's been takin' up karate for over thirty years. I think Kim said that he was some kind of priest, or monk, or somethin'! It's a religion to 'em.

RANDALL

You're really into that stuff, huh?

RANDY

(*Becomes sullen.*)

It teaches me how ta fight back! No one picks on me anymore.

(*Lowers his head, and looks at his hands.*)

RANDALL

(*Feeling Randy's change of attitude.*)

I'm sorry that I never had the time to teach you how to fight. I hadda work so damn hard!

RANDY

(*Unwilling to accept what was just said to him.*)

Umm. Famous last words! No one ever has the time for me.

RANDALL

(*Desperately trying to change the subject and the prevailing attitude.*)

So, how's school?

(*Expressed with more enthusiasm that seems necessary.*)

RANDY

Okay…I guess.

RANDALL

How are your marks?

RANDY

Above average. I gotta double promotion last year. I do alotta readin' on my own.

RANDALL

(*Seeing an opening.*)
Oh, yeah! What do ya read?

RANDY

Anythin' I can get. When the teachers pass out the text books at the beginnin' of the year, I read 'em all the way through in the first week! That's how I jumped a grade last year… readin' so much.

RANDALL

I'm way behind in my reading. I used to read alot too, once.
(*Looks Randy up and down.*)
Boy, you're growing fast! You're almost as big as me! Stand up and let me look at you.
(*Randy gets to his feet, expressionlessly.*)
You are bigger than me!
(*Randy sits back down. Moments pass in silence.*)
I came by today just to see you.
(*Randy doesn't respond.*)
Your mother told me before that you didn't want me to come up and visit you.

RANDY

I never said that! I thought you didn't want ta see <u>me</u>!

RANDALL

(*Unmoved.*)

Your mother doesn't lie Randy. Why didn't you want me to come and see you? I'm your father, Randy.

RANDY

(*Becomes extremely emotional.*)

I never said that I didn't wanna see you! She told me that you wanted ta come…but ya never came!

RANDALL

(*Not believing Randy, sighs.*)

You know the separation was not all my fault… I hadda go before I went crazy.

(*Reaches a hand in his coat pocket, and brings out a pack of cigarettes and a book of matches.*)

You want one?

(*Offers a cigarette to Randy.*)

RANDY

(*Looks at the cigarette, shaking his head from side to side.*)

No…I don't smoke.

RANDALL

(*Disbelieving Randy.*)

That's what you tell your mother…I know better. Here!

(*Pushing the pack of cigarettes closer to Randy.*)

RANDY

(*Practically pleading with Randall to believe him.*)

I don't smoke, Daddy! I'm in trainin'.

RANDALL

(*Forcefully.*)

Here!

(*Pushing the pack of cigarettes even closer to Randy. Randy sighs, then takes the offered cigarette. They both light up, but Randy doesn't smoke his. He just sits watching the cigarettes burn down in his hand.)*

I wanted to come back a number of times, but your mother said that you kids didn't want me to.

(Looks at Randy, sorrowfully.)

You see, I hadda lot of pressures on me. Working two jobs is hard! Being a colored man in this country is hard, especially if you want to keep your dignity. When the fire came it almost pushed me over the brink... the bills piled up sky high. And I guess I took a lot of my frustrations on you kids and your mother. When you get a little older you'll understand better what I'm sayin'...you'll have a family of your own then.

RANDY

(Moved by what his father just said to him, answers sadly.)

Nobody blames you, Daddy.

RANDALL

(Speaking, as if he never heard Randy.)

I always wanted to come back...but I didn't because you all didn't want me to.

(Tears well up in Randall's eyes. He wipes his eyes with the sleeve of his coat, and sniffles a couple of times.)

I've gotta cold!

(Silence for a few seconds.)

Why didn't you want me to come and see you?

RANDY

(Becomes angry.)

I never said that! Why doesn't anybody ever believe what I say?!

(Begins to cry.)

You wasn't even listenin' ta me! You never did - nobody does! Where were <u>you</u> when I needed you?!

(Randy jumps to his feet, runs down the steps, and out of the scene to the left of the stage. Randall remains seated on the porch. He puts his elbows on his thighs, and his head in his hands. He sits looking vacantly out over the audience.. .tears begin to fall from his eyes. The curtain slowly closes.)

END OF PLAY

NARRATION AS CURTAIN SLOWLY DROPS

From his childhood, society drills into man's head
that he must struggle alone to acquire life's daily bread.
And woman's position is thus clearly defined
to be one step ahead of man, yet four steps behind!

There isn't enough room for husband and wife to grow,
and within this vacuum they must reap what they sow.
So, in mortal combat, these two lost souls abide—
separated by egoism, fear, and foolish pride.

Their children would watch in horror and despair;
as strife and physical violence pulled apart their parental pair.
The parents couldn't see from their children's tears—
how their separation would affect the children in later years.

So, you want to build a home!
Is your foundation sunk on stone?
Because, if life doesn't settle like it should;
time will find a tinderbox where a family once stood...
                gone, gone house of wood.

ABOUT THE AUTHOR

Ralph C Hamm III

Ralph, born in 1950, is serving a non-capital first offense life sentence for "intent," stemming from a criminal episode that occurred in 1968 – when he was seventeen years old. During his decades of imprisonment he has aided in spearheading Massachusetts' prison reform movement, has earned degrees in liberal arts, divinity, metaphysics, and paralegal; as well as developed into a published poet, playwright, musician, and artist. In 2007 he was acknowledged as a contributor to the book, *When the Prisoners Ran Walpole* by Jamie Bissonette; and is author of *Manumission: The Liberated Consciousness of a Prison(er) Abolitionist*, as well as *Blackberry Juice*.

WHY DO I WRITE?

I write because a prison needs a poet—a chronicler—someone who has experienced at firsthand the agony of the disenfranchised, and can interpret through his very soul the expression of suffering by the collective whole.

I write because the only way for the public to learn about what it is like to sub-exist within "the bowels of the beast" (the criminal justice system) is to listen to an inhabitant. Not just any inhabitant, but one who understands and can articulate the conditions of his confinement. No criminal psychologist, sociologist, so-called criminal justice professional, nor salaried correctional official knows what it is truly like to venture through the looking-glass of the criminal justice system as a member of the marginalized under-caste in America – unless they have served time themselves.

I write because the Massachusetts Parole Board has told me, after having served over 40 years on a non-capital life sentence, to die in prison because of my beliefs.

I write because I refuse to quietly go to my grave.

I write because my life was offered as a sacrifice upon the altar of criminal justice: as the means to secure and uphold an easy and speedy conviction—to curry favor and gratitude from a race-conscious and vindictive society—to secure a method in the Commonwealth to undermine the Constitutional guarantees to trial by jury and effective assistance of trial counsel...and to forward the careers of those involved with the so-called professional aspects of the case in the Massachusetts legal system.

I write because criminal justice in Massachusetts is told as a one-sided story: where voices of the poor undercaste are seldom, if ever, heard...where there are no second chances, nor room for redemption.

I write because in Massachusetts the courts have declared that it is "reasonable" for skin color to be the determinant factor in coercing juvenile defendants to waive trial by jury—that trial counsel does not have to investigate the facts of a criminal case if he has access to the prosecutor's case file, in spite of the Massachusetts Canon of Ethics—and, as a result, that physical, material, and exculpatory evidence can be withheld or destroyed prior to trial.

I write because juvenile first time offenders such as myself can receive life sentences for non capital offenses, because he "is black and his victims white" that an adult codefendant, and ringleader of said criminal episode, can enter into a secret sentencing deal with the Commonwealth, testify against and inculcate a juvenile codefendant, and thereby be released from charges against a female victim and returned to the community to commit even more egregious crimes...that victims can be convinced to lie, without having to face cross-examination from trial counsel, because counsel has determined that the victims have been through enough already.

I write because it is the desire of the criminal justice system to have its victims suffer in obscurity, to be tortured away from prying eyes and a possible scrutiny by the mass media; thereby absolving society from any plausible charge of injustice, as well as from the realization that the social conditions that birth criminal behavior are responsible for crime.

I write because America is a country whose social reality is viewed by most through the prism of rose-tinted glasses, after first being distorted by a series of Fun House mirrors and smokescreens...a society where the Voters' Rights Act of 1965 and 1970 must be continually renewed by a sitting President, in an effort to guarantee that black people (the descendants of slaves) maintain their right to vote...a country where one of the by-products of mass incarceration, in several states, is a lifetime of disenfranchisement of the right to vote and the methodology utilized by politicos to circumvent the Voters' Rights Acts.

I write because in spite of America's bombast proclaiming freedom and liberty for all, the 13th Amendment to the U.S. Constitution holds an authorized exception to the abolition of slavery which is rigidly enforced and exploited.

I write because.

WHAT DO I WRITE ABOUT?

I write about how the Massachusetts criminal justice system is criminal to the degree where it is not a system of justice, it is a system of "just-us." The system is designed to fool enough of the general public enough of the time to justify its disparities against racial minorities and the poor. It is a system of "just-us" that reserves its severest penalties and sentences for its lower income/caste members of society, except when the violations of the law are bartered with informants and/or members of organized crime tendered by a rose in a fisted kid glove.

For example, I write about: in what other system of social control can a black juvenile first time offender receive a life sentence for intending to commit a crime, as well as receive a consecutive life sentence for his involvement in a $20.00 robbery of an emphasized white person, and thereby serve over 44 years in prison: while a white organized crime hit-man can confess to killing 22 people, barter and serve only 12 years in prison, and be released back into society as an avowed serial killer; and the black juvenile's trial/defense attorney (as a white member of yet another aspect of organized crime in this State) can rob a client of $100,000.00 from an estate, barter, and not serve one minute in prison?

I write about the benefits of the criminal "just-us" system serving as an economic advantage for the middle and upper castes, and the social institutions at work to maintain rather than eliminate crime – to reinforce the levels of caste in society. Why must crime be maintained? It is essential to have a visible (black) criminal population as a boundary by which to establish a cultural identity in society, and to sustain a solidarity amongst those who share that cultural identity. Criminal "just-us" is nothing more than a system of perpetual regulations and mirages used to marginalize the disenfranchised poor as scapegoats for society's shortcomings.

CPSIA information can be obtained at www.ICGtesting.com
Printed in the USA
BVOW03s0817060913

330195BV00004B/6/P

9 781935 656807